Five-Star Reviews For
Temptation: Rendezvous with God Volume Two

Relatable

"Bill Myers is a master ~~~~~~~~~~~~~~
stories. *Temptation* is ev ~~~~~~~~~~~
forces us to accept that ~~~~~~~~~~ through this
tightly-woven account, he deftly shows our own failures,
and though his characters get muddied up in the process,
the reader gets a sense of satisfaction that it (almost—
sequels coming) ends the way it should." —Sam Hall

As always . . . a powerful tale of faith and God's Presence!

"A challenging story filled with Our Lord's Presence in
a mixture of anxiety, challenges, growing faith, and Our
Lord's Presence and Healing Love in the midst of it all!"
—Cricketj77

Easy read that hits hard

"The first *Rendezvous with God* was great but more geared
toward a skeptic or agnostic. This, however, hits squarely in
the chest of any Christian who is struggling through any
kind of trial. Frankly, I was upset with the book more than
once, which for anyone who's ever heard a good convicting
sermon knows exactly what that means. The message Bill
conveys is a timeless one in a modern context while never
feeling preachy. If I had to nitpick anything, it would be
the main character can be a bit of an idiot (specifically

when speaking with the opposite sex), but I've also met some guys like that, so it's not unrealistic.

"One thing to note is the exact situation the main character gets embroiled in is a *very* hot button and real issue facing many people today. I found his reactions to those specific circumstances to be very relatable, and I found Bill's devotion questions at the end of the book to be very helpful in processing through that, as well as many of the deeper theological issues that arose as well.

"TLDR: I would highly recommend this book to *any* Christian, as it hits very hard in the heart but is completely approachable with likable characters you can identify with and root for." —Benjamin C. Reese

Like fine chocolate for my soul!

"I am reading *Temptation* slowly so that I can savor every word, like fine chocolate for my soul. I'm going to be desperate for more when I'm done and am hoping Bill Myers will keep writing." —Sherrie Eldridge

Second book in a very unusual story

"This series has to be the most different story we've read. It's a bit unusual using real historical events out of the first century. Mixing current events with accounts from the culture of the Middle East during the life of the prophet Yeshua, truth is woven into the life of the main character. The title is exactly what the story confronts head-on in so many ways, lives, and outcomes. It would be best, if possible, to read the first volume before this one. The two are one story." —eaglegrafix

COMMUNE

COMMUNE

Rendezvous with God – Volume Three

Bill Myers

FIDELIS
PUBLISHING

*Discussion questions have been included
to facilitate personal and group study.*

Fidelis Publishing®
Sterling, VA • Nashville, TN
www.fidelispublishing.com

ISBN: 9781956454246
ISBN: 9781956454253 (ebook)

Commune (Rendezvous with God – Volume Three)

Order at www.faithfultext.com for a significant discount. Email info@ fidelispublishing.com to inquire about bulk purchase discounts.

Unless otherwise indicated, all Scripture comes from Holy Bible, New International Version®, NIV® Copyright ©1973, 1978, 1984, 2011 by Biblica, Inc.® Used by permission. All rights reserved worldwide.

Published in association with Amaris Media International

Cover designed by Diana Lawrence
Interior design by LParnell Book Services
Edited by Amanda Varian

Manufactured in the United States of America

10 9 8 7 6 5 4 3 2 1

Craig Sturges:

Humble, self-sacrificing warrior.

∽

"Find out about prayer.
Somebody must find out about prayer."

Albert Einstein

∽

PART ONE

CHAPTER
ONE

"OH, LOOK AT that. What a lovely surprise. You know, I bet not everyone can produce something like this. I mean, look at that. And the creamy smooth texture. That's really something."

Amber, my fourteen-year-old niece, and I were into Week Two of raising her newborn, little Billie-Jean. And we were following the baby books to the letter—well, what we managed to remember in our sleep-deprived states. And, "Since you can never start too early in deepening the child-parent bond and building your child's self-esteem," we celebrated each and every diaper disaster as if it were a major piece of art.

"You've really got a talent, young lady," I said. "I couldn't be prouder."

Not only did this increase Billie-Jean's self-esteem, but forcing myself to view her work with a positive spin had all but eliminated my rookie retchings.

The good news was by today I'd clearly managed to distinguish the front of the diaper from the back, so do-overs were no longer an issue. Why they're not clearly labeled with an F and B is beyond me. The bad news was as I removed the masterpiece and set it too close, her little hand darted into the goop. "Billie Je—" She flung it high into the air, "Bill—" and turned my white sweatshirt into modern, splatter-art. "Come on, are you serious?"

But as the devoted student, I immediately checked my tone and found something to praise. "That's quite an arm you have there." I smiled as I wiped my neck with the back of my wrist—as she ran her hand through her hair. (Alright, this time I did throw up, but just a little in my mouth.)

I'd like to say Amber and I had settled into a routine. But that would imply we had goals and knew what we were doing. We didn't. Not in the slightest. For me, success was getting more than two hours sleep at a time, any time, day or night. And, yes, I'll admit Amber and I played possum, pretending to be asleep so the other would have to come to Billie-Jean's rescue. Unfortunately, Amber wasn't pretending. The poor kid was beyond exhaustion. Me too. I don't want to trivialize the tortures of waterboarding, but force any Enemy of the State to spend two weeks taking care of a newborn and let's see how soon they start talking.

When it came to crying, there was no end to the baby books' advice—and to their contradictions. Some said, pick her up when she's crying. Others said, leave her and teach her independence. Others insisted the child should be rocked. While others said, scoop her up every time she whimpers and lay her down every time she stops. Following that last piece of advice meant I could cancel my gym membership which I never use anyway.

Amber, for her part, took to parenting like a duck to water. For the first time in her adolescent life, she realized there was someone in the world other than herself. That didn't mean she didn't slack when she could, but for the first time since she moved in with me last Christmas I saw the faintest seeds of responsibility taking root.

And breastfeeding? She loved it. And not just because she now had a "hot figure" to show off. She loved the whole process. While I—well let's just say there were times my middle-aged sensibilities redefined the term *awkward*.

To my credit, just once and only once I ventured to ask, "Have you ever thought of bottle feeding?"

"You're kidding me," she scorned. "You know the trauma, the emotional scarring that causes and how it follows a person through their whole, entire life?"

"I was bottle-fed."

She gave me a look. Point made.

Anyway, after cleaning Billie-Jean, "Wasn't that exciting? Aren't we having fun?" the next step involved getting her into her little outfit with its dozen microscopic snaps that must be snapped in exactly the right order. Like the diapers, labeling would be appreciated, maybe color coding, anything to prevent us sausage-finger-types from finally completing the task only to discover we were off by one snap and would have to start over.

I don't want to say Billie-Jean took over my life. That ship sailed last Christmas when Amber moved in. Now I was just looking for scraps of wreckage to cling to:

- Moments I could collapse onto the sofa, or chair (or floor)
- Finding respite in my treasured, first edition books—though it meant climbing across the mountains of unused baby gifts that had taken over my library/ex-bedroom
- Or just finding a job.

Not that losing work was the baby's fault. I managed to accomplish that all on my own—shooting my mouth off to a press that twisted my words to sound as if I blamed the victim of an alleged rape.

After the campus demonstration against me—and yes, there was a demonstration—the university was smart enough to put me on a leave of absence until things cooled down. The problem was things weren't cooling down. After Sean's suicide (the alleged perpetrator and my best friend), things only grew worse. Student protests grew louder and larger. Within days I'd not only become Sean's proxy for their outrage, but the poster child for every sexist/misogynist of my generation. In short, I'd put my foot in it—all the way to my neck. Earlier, when Yeshua said he would free me of finding self-worth in what people thought, he wasn't kidding. It's hard to find self-worth when you have zero market value as a human being.

And my work?

"We've seen the news footage, we've read the transcripts," Dr. DeVos, the Vice-Chancellor said earlier by phone. *By phone*, because my presence on campus was too hot an issue. "And since you've broken no law or morality clause, the tenure committee feels there are no grounds for dismissal—technically."

"Technically?" I said.

"Will, the media isn't letting go of this one. Nor is the academic community. I'm receiving calls and e-mails from universities across the country. And from more than one local politician."

"What exactly are you saying?"

He paused, then continued. "We can't fire you. We don't want to fire you. But every day you stay on faculty, our reputation is dragged further into the mud. The registrar's office says we're already experiencing a decrease in next year's enrollment."

"Because of me?"

More silence.

"So," I tried keeping an even voice, "you're suggesting what? That I should quit?"

"That's your decision, Will. We'll do all we can for you at this end. But I know you love and believe in this institution as much as we do. So, I—well, as I said, it's your decision."

The conversation had been last Tuesday. And forty-eight hours ago I sent in my letter of resignation, complete with sleep-depraved typos. It was a grand gesture which everyone applauded and thought noble. It was also foolish, leaving me no source of income or unemployment insurance—something that would come in handy for my mortgage, the alimony to Cindy (as she and her boy toy continued touring the world), and the astronomical medical bills for Billie-Jean's dramatic entrance into the world.

Yeshua also said I'd be free of defining myself through what I did for a living and how much money I made. So far, he was three for three.

And maybe he had a point. Because at this moment, none of those mattered. Not in comparison to this amazing new life gurgling and cooing at me from the changing table. I was working on my third round of aligning the snaps when my cell rang. Caller ID said it was Patricia Swenson, the faculty member who along with Darlene helped me deliver Billie-Jean in Amber's wrecked car.

"Do you mind if I get that?" I asked.

Billie-Jean blew a snot bubble as consent.

I checked my hands, pulled out the phone, and wedged it against my shoulder. "Hey, Patricia."

"Hello, Will. How are we today?"

"Oh, pretty good. I think I squeezed in a couple hours of sleep since we last spoke. What was that, yesterday? Hard to keep track of time with all the—"

"I meant the baby, Will."

"Oh, right. She's doing fine too." I scooted the used diaper just a little further from Billie Jean's reach. "She does a lot of fussing, but I guess that's normal."

"How's she eating?"

"Like a horse. Poor thing can't decide whether to eat or breathe."

"What does that mean?"

"After a gulp or two she comes up gasping."

There was no response.

"That's normal too," I said. "Right?"

"How's her color?"

"Always the doctor," I joked.

"How's her color?"

"Funny you should ask." I reached for Billie-Jean's tiny hand. "This morning I noticed her fingernails were kind of purple."

"Purple?"

"Yes. I just figured—"

"And her lips? Their color?"

I looked down at her. "Mostly white." I leaned closer. "Actually, they're more a faint blue. Is that a problem?"

"Alright," she said, "there's no need to panic, but I want you to bundle Billie-Jean up and catch the next ferry to the mainland."

"You want me to—"

"Tell Ambrosia not to worry, but you two need to get the baby to a doctor. Today."

"We don't have an appointment."

"I'll make sure you get in."

"It's that serious?"

"Not yet."

"Then—"

"Do it, Will. Trust me. Just do it."

CHAPTER
TWO

"BLANKETS?"

"Check."

"Extra clothes?"

"Check." As Amber buckled into the front seat she said, "I don't know why she's being so mysterious."

"She just doesn't want us to worry."

"Right . . . *'Get her to a doctor today.'* Like I'm not going to worry."

Of course, Amber had a point. For us, a huge one. If Billie-Jean so much as burped funny, we hit the baby books. And her poop? More often than not we searched it like tea leaves looking for a sign. Granted, Patricia was strung tighter than a Stradivarius, particularly when it came to religion. But when it came to medicine, she knew her stuff. And with far more letters after her name than mine, we took her suggestion seriously. Of course, this meant leaving the house for the first time with Billie-Jean, which meant packing up enough stuff to go to the moon. Hence, the NASA checklist:

"Diapers?"

"Check."

"Wipes."

"Check."

"Spit-up cloth? Diaper bag? Carrier?"

"Yes! Yes! Yes!" Amber cried impatiently. "Can we please just go?"

"Car seat?"

"Do you really have to ask?"

Another good point. Between the two of us it took forty minutes to get it locked into the seat—quite an accomplishment considering neither of us had a degree in mechanical engineering.

"*Please* . . .?" she repeated.

I dropped the car into gear. "If we forgot anything, we can pick it up on the mainland."

But I'd barely pulled away before she cried, "Stop!"

"What is it now?"

"The baby! We forgot the baby!"

&

We were halfway to the mainland. I stood at the railing of the ferry, breathing in the cool, salty air of spring. And praying. Lots and lots of praying. Amber opted to stay in the car, making sure Billie-Jean didn't die after each breath. I knew calling Patricia again and asking her to speculate what might be wrong was a waste of time. That wasn't her style. The only absolute Patricia Swenson swore by was the Bible—which she knew cover to cover. (What Yeshua meant a few weeks back when he said I would be her teacher was beyond me.)

The thought barely surfaced when I felt a hot breeze against my back. I turned and saw Yeshua a dozen yards away. He sat on a grassy hill overlooking the lake we'd met at so many times before. Surrounding him was a handful of men including Peter, the big guy with the big mouth, along with John and James who'd been with him on the mountain when God made his guest appearance with Moses and Elijah.

Below us, down on the beach, a large crowd looked up, apparently waiting for Yeshua to come down and join them. But for now, it appeared to be a private session, just him and the boys. Shading his eyes, he spotted me and motioned for me to join the group. Others turned to see who he looked at, but of course they couldn't see me. They never did. He motioned again and I started through the knee-high grass toward them. But, feeling like an interloper, I stayed to the side, practicing my version of social distancing.

As I arrived, he resumed speaking to the group. "And when you pray, don't keep babbling on like the pagans who think they'll be heard because of their many words."

I winced. Hadn't I just been doing that very thing on the ferry—praying over and over again, thinking I'd somehow wear God down with all my verbiage?

"Don't be like them," he repeated, "because your Father knows what you need before you even ask him."

It was a strange comment. I mean, if God already knows what we need, why bother asking him in the first place?

Yeshua continued, "This then is how you should pray. 'Our Father in heaven.'" As he spoke, his voice grew quieter, more intense. "Hallowed be your name." He waited a moment for some reaction. When it was clear there was none, he continued. "Your kingdom come. Your will be done on earth as it is in heaven." Again, he paused. And again, he was met with blank, blinking faces. If he was discouraged, he didn't let on. "Give us this day our daily bread." Another pause. Someone coughed. He took a breath and pushed on. "Forgive us our debts as we forgive our debtors." One final pause before he wrapped up with, "Lead us not into temptation but deliver us from evil."

I'd heard the prayer a dozen times in my life, but it was entirely different, listening to him speak with such conviction. And yet, instead of a rousing reception, he was met with polite nods, more on autopilot than enthusiasm, along with the obligatory murmuring of, "Amen."

Except Peter. He seemed legitimately puzzled. "I'm sorry, Teacher . . . At the beginning, when you started off, you said, 'Our *father*'?"

"That's right."

"Father, as in . . . *father*? *Papa?*"

Yeshua nodded.

Peter frowned, turned to the group, wondering if they'd heard what he heard. As he waited, lights slowly came on, uneasy looks were shared. Two or three leaned to each other and quietly whispered.

Yeshua watched, obviously pleased they were starting to think. And the more they thought, the more puzzled they became. Rising, he brushed the grass from his robe and started toward me. I threw a nervous look to the men, then realized he was doing his slow-motion thing with them—or his fast-forward thing with us. Either way, they weren't frozen, just moving like the minute hand of a clock.

"Hey, Will." He arrived and threw his arms around me. The embrace felt good and was definitely needed. "How've you been?"

When we separated I shrugged, "Oh, you know."

He grinned. "Yes, I do. So, how's the baby?"

"You've heard what's going on with her, right?"

"Of course. She's part of your next season."

"Season?" I asked, my suspicions already rising.

"Of growth, remember? Or at least part of it."

"Which . . . part?"

He chuckled and nodded to the group. "The part on prayer, of course."

I looked back to the men. "They weren't exactly impressed, were they."

"Sometimes it takes a while for them."

"Except the 'Our Father,' part," I said. "That raised a few eyebrows."

He turned back to the group. "Sad, isn't it? After all this time, all these centuries, people still don't understand the Father's love for his children."

"Easy for you to say." He turned to me and I answered, "You *are* his Son."

His eyes twinkled then focused with a gentle intensity. "And so are you, my brother. So are you."

He waited and I shifted under his gaze, knowing full well he referred to the bloody murder I'd seen so many months before, the sacrifice on another hill that made it all possible.

He continued more softly. "Everyone prays, Will. Sadly, most don't know who they're praying to."

"It does feel a little weird," I admitted, looking out over the lake. "All that intimacy. And, like you said, if he already knows what we want, why even bother asking?"

"Which is why we're about to enter your next season. If you're willing."

"On prayer?"

"Few things are more important." He waited for me to look back to him. "I know you agreed earlier to continue, but this one is going to be rough; you'll have to hang on tight. And if you want to back out, now's the time; I'll fully understand."

"Will it hurt?"

"What was it your track coach used to shout, 'No pain, no gain'?"

"It's going to hurt."

He smiled. "Pain is necessary if you want to grow. But suffering—that's optional."

I didn't understand what he meant but what else was new? The point is, he'd given me a chance to reconsider—especially now with a potentially sick baby and the loss of work (not to mention loss of reputation). I could back out, take the easy way, play it safe, and what—miss the adventure he had planned for me? Sit back and do what? Slowly stagnate? Atrophy? Or I could take the risk and say yes. So far, he'd never let me down, at least in the long run. It was always confusing, but he always came through. Which brought up the other issue—the bond forming between us. It was deeper than trust, or faith or anything people called religious. Don't get me wrong, I wouldn't be going out and buying him flowers, but something happened to us. To me. He said I had a choice, but in truth, there was no choice. Not when considering the depth of my feelings—or my trust. He only wanted the best for me. I knew that. So, with a deep breath, I looked to the ground and slowly began to nod.

I felt his hand gently rest on my shoulder. Neither of us said a word; none was necessary. When he did speak, his voice had a slight catch. "Well then, my friend . . ." He cleared his throat. "We'll talk soon."

I nodded.

He turned and started for the group, but not before adding, "You'll be amazed at the growth."

Not exactly excited, I repeated, "Growth."

"And freedom."

Unable to hide my sarcasm, I added. "Like the last time?"

He looked back over his shoulder and grinned. "Even better."

CHAPTER
THREE

SEASON OF GROWTH? He wasn't kidding. And he wasted little time.

"Why are we slowing?" Amber called from the back seat where she sat with Billie-Jean. "What are you doing?"

"I'm trying not to hit the guy in front of us."

"So go around."

"There is no going around. Even the emergency lane is full."

"Well, do something."

I did. I sat there praying, trapped in the car with the two of them—Amber in a panic meltdown, Billie-Jean thinking it was a good time to break her record for perpetual crying.

"Uncle Will!"

Seventy more minutes passed before we reached the front of the line and were directed around a tanker that had dumped its 11,000 gallons of milk across the freeway.

"Let's go!" Amber shouted, rewaking Billie-Jean who decided to try and beat her recently acquired record.

"Well, okay, if you say so. No use crying over spilled milk."

Amber's silence was deafening.

My second opportunity for *growth* came at the office of Dr. O.S. Kanney's; a pediatrician in Everett. Patricia said he was the best and she'd pulled several strings to get us in for an appointment. Unfortunately, the young receptionist who greeted us was as clueless as she was courteous.

"What do you mean he's not available?" I demanded. Between Billie-Jean's cryfest, Amber's nagging, and the two-hour confinement in the car, my patience was pretty much shot. More importantly, this was Amber's baby we were talking about.

To her credit, the receptionist politely explained, "I'm so sorry, but he is at the hospital, making rounds."

"We had an appointment."

She examined the chart before her. "Yes, I see you do. At 1:40. Unfortunately, it is now 3:10 and—"

"There was a tanker spill on I-5. We got here as soon as we could. When will he be back?"

"If you'd like I can schedule you first thing tomorrow morning."

"Tomorrow morning!"

"I really am sorry. But that's the best we—"

"Do you see this baby?"

She rose to look over the counter at Billie-Jean who had worn herself out and was sleeping it off in Amber's baby carrier. "Ohh," the receptionist cooed. "She's sooo sweet."

"Her color," I said.

"She looks a little pale."

"Pale?" I said. "Pale! Where is he?"

"Pardon me?"

"What hospital is he at?"

"Well, today he's at Cascade Valley in Arlington. But I'm afraid you can't—"

I spun around to Amber, "C'mon," and started for the door.

"Uncle Will—"

Amber had never seen me so worked up—except the time the drug dealer at our New Year's Eve party experienced my rage—a wrath which only succeeded in landing me in the nearest ER. I took her arm, perhaps a bit too forcefully, which jarred the baby carrier, which woke Billie-Jean who immediately began her glass-shattering screams.

"Sir!" the receptionist called after us.

"Uncle Will!"

Once on the road, Amber did her best to calm me down. And, no, I didn't miss the irony—my fourteen-year-old niece, the poster child for drama queens, trying to calm *me* down. But Billie-Jean was going to see the doctor and she was going to see him today.

Thirty minutes later we arrived at the Arlington hospital—with a receptionist far more professional than the doctor's receptionist, making her even less helpful. From behind the desk, she looked up at me through jewel-framed bifocals. "Dr. Kanney?" she said. "Yes, he's here, but he's making rounds."

"Right, I understand," I said. "But we have to see him."

"He's visiting a patient."

"Right. But our baby is sick, we have to see him."

"He's making rounds and visiting a patient."

"I know he's—" I caught myself, took a breath, and brought it down a few degrees. "I know he's making rounds, I know he's visiting a patient, but our baby is very sick. Can you tell me which one?"

"Which patient?"

"Yes, what room."

"Are you a patient of his?"

"No, yes, I mean we will be. Can you just tell me the room?"

"As a patient you should visit him in his office."

"We tried. Take a look at this child. Her fingers. We need to see him.

"Then, I suggest re-scheduling."

"I—just—where is he?"

"As I said, he's with a patient."

"I know he's . . . I took another breath. "What patient? What room number?"

"If you wish to see the doctor, you need to call his office and make—"

"Forget it!" I spun from the desk and stared down the hall. "I'll find him myself."

"Uncle Will—"

"Stay right here. I'll find him and bring him back."

"But—"

"Your baby needs a doctor and we're going to get a doctor. So just wait—"

"Sir . . ."

"—right here and we'll be back."

"Sir!"

I headed down the hall.

"Okay—Father," I muttered, "*Our Father*. Right now you're zero for two. This would be a good time to come through and prove yourself."

The good news was the hospital was relatively small, with only forty-eight beds. The bad news was it had the security of San Quentin. Within moments, I heard another, more commanding voice, call after me, "Sir. Sir!"

A quick glance over my shoulder revealed a young, uniformed guard.

"I'm looking for Dr. Kanney," I said, poking my head into one patient's room, then continuing down the hall.

"You need to come with me."

"Right. As soon as I find Dr. Kanney. I just need—"

"Now."

"In a minute." I checked another room. "I just have to—"

I heard footsteps and before I could turn, a pair of hands grabbed my arms. "Sir, I need you to—"

I tried shrugging them off. "You don't understand, I need—"

His grip grew firmer. "Sir."

I squirmed harder but he was obviously not getting the message. I turned to explain and was surprised to see how snug the uniform fit his biceps. "I'm afraid there's been some miscommunication," I said. "I just need to find—"

He tried throwing me into some sort of hold which I'd have none of. It was more accident than intentional, but—accident or not—during our brief struggle my elbow flew up and inadvertently hit his nose with such force he stumbled backward, bringing us to an entirely new level of communication . . . involving my eyes burning with pepper spray and being shoved face-first against the wall as my hands were cuffed in plastic restraints. There was plenty of blood. Just not mine.

Despite my apologies and attempts to explain, he escorted me back down the hall, through the lobby and out the door toward an arriving squad car complete with flashing lights.

Amber followed, shouting, "Uncle Will!"

I did my best to explain. "I'm telling you, this is all a misunderstanding; you don't need to—"

"Uncle Will!"

"That's my niece. Her baby. All we need is to see the doctor. This is just a silly misunderstanding."

I presented the same case to the police officer who took charge and opened the back door of his car. "It's all a misunderstanding. Trust me, just a big, misunderstanding." The fact the hospital guard stood nearby, holding a blood-soaked towel against his bleeding nose did not help my cause.

"Uncle Will!" Amber followed behind with Billie-Jean who, now awake, enthusiastically screamed her own concerns.

"Watch your head, sir," the officer shouted over the noise as he lowered me into the back seat—as yet another voice joined the chorus:

"Will! Will!"

I looked through the side window to see Patricia leaping from her car and running toward us.

"What have you done this time?"

CHAPTER
FOUR

WHEN YESHUA SHOWED up in my jail cell wearing his signature white robe and sandals, I simply glanced to him. "Glad to see you could make it," I said. I wasn't being snarky. Well, okay, maybe a little. But if what he previously said about loving us the same on our best days as on our worst—well, here was his golden opportunity.

"No problem," he answered as he sat on the cot beside me. "Friends always show up for friends."

"A tad late, wouldn't you say?" Alright, that was snarky. And I winced. What business did I have talking to God the Son like that?

But he took it all in stride. "By my schedule, I'm right on time."

I let it go. If I'd learned anything over the months, it's our schedules seldom match. Neither do our agendas—at least in the beginning.

For the past ninety minutes I'd been cooling my heels in the Arlington City Jail. My hosts were polite enough and the accommodations weren't bad—though it won't be getting five stars on my Yelp review—unless I take a sudden liking to cinderblock walls and the smell of disinfectant.

I dropped my head and shook it. "How could I have been so stupid?"

"Lots of practice?"

If I looked up, I'm sure I'd see his trademark twinkle. I might have even smiled back. But at the moment, I was too busy wallowing in my default position: self-pity.

As always, he waited, letting me stew and stare at the floor, until I mumbled, "I don't know how it happened."

"Love," he answered.

I continued, "It's like I was this crazy madman."

"Love," he repeated.

"The way I treated the receptionist—both of them," I shook my head. "And the thing with the security guard."

"Love."

I finally looked to him and he continued, "What do you think the Father's wrath and anger is all about?"

I frowned. "You're saying it's love?"

"It's the same coin, just the other side."

"That makes no sense. How can God's wrath have anything to do with his love?"

He rose to his feet. "Got a second?"

I looked around the cell as the obvious answer.

He reached down to my hand. "Let me show you something."

"Here?"

"No." Helping me to my feet, he said, "Here."

Instantly, we stood in a courtyard surrounded by tall, white, limestone walls. We'd been here once or twice before. There were always people, but nothing close to the crowd I now saw. Off to our right, stretched a dozen wood tables, men sitting and standing on both sides, shouting and bartering. To our left, stood row after row of wooden pens full of bleating sheep and bellowing cattle—along with their accompanying flies and the stench of manure. While at the far back wall rose stacks of wooden cages crammed with living birds: doves, by the look of it.

But it was Yeshua who caught my attention. Not the Yeshua beside me—he was still there—but the one storming through the pens, throwing open their gates and driving out the animals.

"What's going on?" I shouted over the commotion. "Is this you clearing the temple?"

The Yeshua beside me nodded.

"But if you're here, how can you be there?"

"Check with Patricia's pastor."

"The theoretical physicist?"

"In the meantime—" He motioned to his other self as the owners of the animals threatened and screamed, while being careful to stay clear of the cord he was swinging in his hand. "Do you see the similarity?"

"Similarity?" I shouted.

"Yours and mine—the anger and rage?"

"Your God's Son," I yelled, "you can get away with it!"

He pointed to dozens of peasants off to our left. "And those are my Father's children." Without further word, he started through the crowd toward them.

"Wait a minute, hang on!" I shouted as I worked my way through the teaming crowd and caught up to him. "I don't understand. I thought you were mad because these guys were making money off God."

"What do I care about that?" he said as we weaved our way through the throng. "I'm furious because my brothers and sisters are being swindled." We slowed to a stop beside a poor young couple—her face already leathered by sun, his back already growing stooped. "I'm outraged because these, my most helpless, are the most abused."

There was a loud crash followed by panicked screams and cries. We spun around to see the other Yeshua had just upended one of the tables, thrown the merchants' scales to the ground, their coins scattering across the floor.

"*Furious? Outraged?* Those are strong words," I shouted.

He motioned to the couple. "Every Passover, these two and thousands like them, travel for days out of love and devotion to offer me a sacrifice. The rich bring sheep and cattle. And the poor, who can barely make ends meet, bring a dove."

Another table crashed—its merchants cursing and shouting—while scrambling away from the madman and his whip.

Yeshua continued, "But the doves they bring from home are never good enough. The temple officials always find flaws, forbidding them to be sacrificed, insisting they buy one of the temple's own birds at an exorbitant price."

"The religious bilking the poor out of money."

He nodded. "And when they try purchasing one of the 'approved' doves, they're told their money isn't holy enough. They must exchange it for temple money which is also inflated at impossible rates." He watched the young couple, his eyes tender and full of pity. "What is intended as an act of love turns into flagrant abuse."

The other Yeshua interrupted. "My house will be called a house of prayer for the nations!" He threw over another table, its money clattering to the ground. "But you've made it a den of thieves!"

As I watched, I began to understand. "So, your anger, it's based on your . . . love."

"Yes. Our *Father's* love. And today, with your niece, you tasted some of that love. You went about it wrong, 'those who live by the sword die by the sword,' but the passion you felt, was identical to my passion and the passion of our . . ." He waited for me to complete the thought.

". . . Father in heaven."

He nodded as we watched his double tearing down the stacked crates of birds and shouting, "Get these out of here!"

"A father's love," I repeated.

"And a mother's." Though he quoted quietly, I heard every word: "'*Can a mother forget the baby at her breast and have no compassion on the child she has borne? Though she may forget, I will not forget you!*'" I looked to him as he turned his palms toward me to reveal their holes—rose-colored scar tissue having never completely filled them—as he finished the quote, "'*See, I have engraved you on the palms of my hands.*'"

Suddenly I was back in my cell—the scene gone, as was he. Gone, but not the lesson:

"Our . . . *Father.*"

FIVE

WITH MORNING'S COFFEE in hand, I shuffled back to my bedroom/laundry room/office. Passing Amber's room, I slowed to a stop. Soft light, diffused by fog, filtered through the window onto the young mother and child. Yeshua's words floated up into me as Amber, eyes closed, slowly rocked the nursing Billie-Jean. *Can a mother forget the baby at her breast and have no compassion on the child she has borne?* There was something deep here. More than love. A oneness. Although Billie-Jean left Amber's womb a week ago, every cell of her body was Amber's. All of her food and nutrients, Amber's. She was Billie-Jean and yet she was Amber. Two people, but one. The metaphor wasn't lost on me. God in us? Us in God? Mother and child, separate but one.

"What are you gawking at?"

Her voice jarred me back to my senses and I averted my gaze. "Sorry."

"You're not turning perv on me, are you?"

"What? No. I, uh—"

She adjusted the baby and covered herself. "I thought you were going to church."

"Right," I said, "church." I resumed my walk down the hall, chastened, but feeling I had caught a glimpse of something eternal. And, as was happening more and more often, wishing I could somehow put it down into words.

As far as church, that was Patricia's suggestion. The fact she'd offered to have any social interaction with me after my media debacle, let alone my scene at the hospital, definitely warranted an early morning trip to the mainland. Dr. Patricia Swenson, head of the school's nursing program, was beautiful in a willowy, fashion-model kind of way. As a missionary kid from Papua New Guinea, she never adapted to what she called the West's relaxed view of sin—which may explain why she had so few friends and why my best friend, Sean, referred to her as the "Ice Lady." She had a moral compass that wouldn't budge and she constantly worked at being the perfect Christian—something a newbie like myself could learn plenty from—making Yeshua's idea that I had something to teach her completely absurd.

The offer to attend church was not her only gift. The day before, she convinced the hospital to drop charges against me while at the same time talking Dr. Kanney into giving a rudimentary checkup of Billie-Jean—which included measuring her O_2 level.

Earlier, as she drove me from the jail back to the hospital to pick up my car, she explained, "The oximeter read 72%. Billie-Jean should be in the 90s."

"Hence the blueness?" I asked.

"And the heart murmur."

"*Heart murmur?* He heard a heart murmur? Why didn't they catch that at her birth?"

"If you recall, it was a busy time."

"So, what's that mean?"

"For starters, it's congenital."

"Congenital? As in birth defect?" She gave no answer and I quietly sighed, "God."

She threw me a look. "I take it that's a prayer?"

I wasn't sure. Swallowing, I asked, "Was it something we did? At the birth should I have . . . Or Amber's OD at Christmas, could that have—"

Patricia cut me off. "It's doubtful. If it's what he thinks, no one's to blame. Roughly one out of 250,000 babies in the US is born with it and for no apparent cause."

"So, we're one of the lucky ones," I muttered. She let it pass. "What do we do?" I asked. "Is it treatable?"

"Absolutely. But first we need to run some tests: EKG, echocardiogram, chest X-ray, and a cardiac catheterization."

I didn't like the sound of the last one. "*Catheterization?*"

"They'll insert a thin tube into her leg and up into her heart to look around."

"She's just a baby," I exclaimed. "Isn't that dangerous?"

She shook her head. "Not really. And it may be necessary to verify our suspicion."

"Of?"

Refusing to speculate, she remained silent.

With rising frustration, I said, "You can at least give me a name. Does it have a name?"

She started to answer, then thought better of it.

I looked out my window and swore again; this time silently. Turning back to her, I asked, "When?"

"It's not an emergency, but the sooner the better. I'll set up an appointment Monday with a pediatric cardiologist down in Seattle. Arguably the best in the state."

"Until then?"

She looked to me.

"It's Saturday afternoon. What are we supposed to do until then?"

"Live your lives as normally as possible."

"Normally?"

"And pray. Prayer is very important."

※

Which was why, beside enjoying her company, I was attending church this morning.

I'd barely finished dressing, this time forgoing the suit and tie—after all, I was told, it is the twenty-first century—when the doorbell rang and Siggy began barking—a clear warning to any intruder they'd be leaped upon and beaten with a wagging tail.

"I'll get it," Amber called.

But I was already down the hall and crossing the kitchen to the door. When I opened it, I came face-to-face with a kid in his late teens complete with peach-fuzz beard, hooded sweatshirt, and stringy black, shoulder-length hair.

"Hello?" I said.

"Hey," he grinned.

"Can I help you?"

"You must be Uncle Will. Super to meet you." He stuck out his hand for a shake.

I didn't offer mine. "And you are?"

Amber chirped from behind. "Hi, Chip."

I turned to see an entirely different Amber—bright, cheery, anything but her usual sullenness—and wearing leggings and a halter top that were too—well, let's just say they were a far cry from her mandatory dress code of sweatshirt and baggy sweats.

His grin widened. "Hey, babe." Then back to me, "I'm Chip Brunswick." Again, he offered his hand. This time I reluctantly shook it.

"I met him at the grocery store," Amber said. "I told you, remember?"

I didn't, which is nothing unusual. Amber started using it as the latest weapon in her adolescent arsenal—pretending we'd talked or I'd given permission for something and then blaming my old age for not remembering.

I turned to him. "And you're here because?"

"We're just going to hang out," Amber said, trying to subtly ease me aside so he could enter. I now understood the leggings and halter top.

But Chip was a pro. Reading my mind, he casually added, "Yeah, we'll probably just go walking on the beach or something."

I held his look, a standoff, until he glanced away. Score one for the old man.

"And practice your lines," Amber added.

"Right," he said.

"Chip is a professional actor. He and his partner are starting a community theater right here on the island."

"A professional," I said, not yielding my position in the doorway. "I didn't know community theater paid."

"Not really," he said, shaking back his hair. "It's kind of a place holder, you know 'til I get discovered and all."

"Exactly how old are you, son?"

"Almost eighteen—though people think I'm a lot older."

"Better hurry," Amber said to me, "or you'll miss the ferry."

"That's right," Chip said. "You're going to church or something, right?"

Glancing to Amber, I said, "Yes, that was the plan."

"So, Jesus can wash away his sins." She laughed, trying harder to nudge me aside. "Cause he's been a naughty boy."

Chip laughed too—a bit high and nervous. Good. The score was now 2–0. "Yeah," he said, "Amber filled me in. Gotta watch that temper, right? I know it's tough when you get older, I mean with declining cognitive skills and all, not to mention those entitled millennials. What pains, right?"

He flipped the hair from his eyes and flashed another smile which I saw no need to return. Doing his best to recover—like I said, he was a pro—he cleared his throat. "Yeah, church. Jesus and stuff. That's good. Old school, but if it works for you, that's cool. Right?"

"Really," I said. "And what exactly is 'new school'?"

"Seriously, you don't want to miss the ferry," Amber said.

Realizing the gloves were off, Chip gracefully rose to the challenge—but nonchalant, cool, and slick. "Oh, the usual, you know, existentialistic responsibility, self-enlightenment, karma—all that stuff. Don't get me wrong, I mean if a person feels they have to dump their junk on some dead dude, that's cool." Another flip of the hair. "Right?" His smile remained constant. The room temperature did not.

"And what exactly do you do with your—*junk*?"

"Me, I take responsibility for it. And if I get it wrong in this life, I just come back the next time to fix it. Or the next, you know, 'til I get it worked out."

"Reincarnation."

"Bingo. You're an educated man, you ought to look into it. The Hindus got some real kick-butt stuff going. You know, meditation, Ayurveda, yoga—"

"Look at the time," Amber said.

"Good point," I said. "Perhaps, when we have more time, you can stay to discuss the deeper ramifications, but for now I have to leave, so thank you for stopping by."

He shot a glance to Amber then back to me. "Right, no, I get it." He reached into his jeans pocket. As he pulled out his billfold, I had the good sense to avoid what I knew to be Amber's death glare.

"Here you go." He produced a card and handed it to me. "That's my business card." Pointing to the bottom, he said, "See it's got my cell, e-mail, address, everything. I'm just six miles up the road. You've got nothing to worry about." Another hair flip. "Right?"

"Besides," Amber said, "Aunt Darlene is coming over."

I turned to her. "Really?"

"In an hour or so. To fix lunch. I told you."

"She'll be fine, Uncle Will—cool if I call you that? I'll keep a careful eye on her and that cute, little rug rat. Right?"

I held his look another moment. This time he did not back down. There was nothing about Chip Brunswick I liked. And from what little I could read, the feeling was mutual. Finally, I reached for my cell.

"What are you doing? Who are you calling?" Amber asked.

"Patricia," I said, entering her number. "To see if we can attend the second service. Darlene should be here by then." As the two exchanged glances, I couldn't resist adding, "Right?"

CHAPTER
SIX

UNLIKE OUR PREVIOUS visit, Patricia made sure we sat as far back in the church/coffeehouse as possible. It was filled with the same small tables lit by candles, the same smell of coffee, and the same college kids. What was not the same were their surprised looks, occasional stares, and a few out-and-out glares by the handful who spotted us. I hoped there might have been a bit more understanding over my media fiasco—considering where we were and all—then again, I was still pretty new to Christianity.

Up front, Dr. Stewart—fifties, sage-looking with a slight Jamaican accent—sat on a stool, casually addressing the packed room.

Earlier, when Darlene failed to show at the house, I gave her a call.

She picked up on the fourth ring, her voice clogged with sleep. "Hello?"

"Hey Darlene, it's Will."

"What time is it?"

"8:30 . . . ish."

I heard another voice mumble in the background and her response. "It's nothing, babe, go back to sleep."

"I'm guessing you're not on the ferry?" I said.

"What? No, it's Sunday, right? I'll be there three or four."

"To fix lunch?"

"No, dinner. Who said anything about lunch?"

"Right. Sorry to wake you."

"No problem." She fumbled with the phone until she disconnected.

I broke the news to Amber who pretended surprise at the miscommunication. So as not to miss the second service, I briskly and a bit abruptly escorted Chip out of the house. To avoid any further miscommunication, I drove behind his yellow Jeep all the way to a room he was renting from some relative before giving him my best and turning to catch the ferry. It was out of my way, but the message was delivered in large font and bold cap letters.

". . . as we continue our studies on the Lord's prayer."

Dr. Stewart's phrase jarred me from my thoughts. Did I hear correctly?

He continued, "By now, I am sure you all understand the '*Our Father*' part—since I have been pounding you over the head with it for weeks."

Soft chuckles rippled through the crowd as I shook my head, once again marveling at Yeshua's cleverness.

"And as far as '*in heaven*,' well, we have discussed that a couple weeks back when I went into my physics rant—how my physicist friends believe we are surrounded by at least eighteen dimensions we cannot see—so I shall not be repeating that."

"Thank you, Jesus!" his heavy-set wife called from the first row of tables—followed by another round of chuckles.

"But what about this next phrase, '*Hallowed be your name*'? Hallowed. Honored. What does that mean, to honor his name? No swearing? I suppose. People do throw his name around like a Frisbee. But look where he puts it in the prayer. At the very beginning. Once I establish who I am praying to—a loving father with unlimited power—my very first request isn't about me. It is about him. His honor. In fact, in the Psalms, when we come into his presence we are instructed to: '*Enter his gates with thanksgiving and his court with praise; give thanks to him and*'—here it comes—'*praise his* name.'

"But why? Is he some egotist, someone so insecure he needs my strokes? Or—as a loving father, is he once again looking out for *my* best interests?"

He paused, letting the question hover over the candle-lit faces.

Clearing his throat, he grew very serious. "I must tell you something, and this is very important. Much of what worship accomplishes is to adjust and realign my soul. It puts my instrument in tune with the rest of the orchestra, with the rest of creation. And, once I am in tune, I see my upcoming requests in an entirely different light. No longer do I beg and grovel at his feet. No longer do I pray *at* him. I begin praying *with* him—in harmony with the perfect will of my all-powerful Father."

The room grew silent. No movement save for the flickering candles.

"Do I always want to do such a thing, to worship? No. That is why the Bible calls it a *sacrifice* of praise. But when I will myself, when I align my soul with the rest of the universe, a peace that passes understanding settles over me; a peace that stands in defiance of my situation. A peace that, though I am surrounded by enemies, allows me to feast at my Father's table—even if I'm in the valley of the shadow of death."

As he spoke, I noticed a light shimmering over our table until it solidified into Yeshua sitting on it. Moving his robe to avoid the candle's flame, he asked, "So how's he doing?"

I gave him a look. "You set all this up, didn't you?"

He shrugged. "Everyone needs a hobby."

"He's good. Though I suspect he had a little help." As I spoke I noticed the closest tables glancing in my direction, some frowning.

"Just *think* the words," Yeshua said. "Remember? Less chance of getting committed that way."

Nodding, I glanced at the nearby students, and thought, *They got an eyeful when Patricia ushered me in.*

Yeshua looked down to her and broke into a warm smile.

I continued, *She'll definitely catch some heat by hanging out with me.*

"Yes, she will." Continuing the smile, he added, "I told you, you'd be crucial in helping her grow."

By ruining her reputation.

"The chains of religion come in all shapes and sizes."

I pretended to understand but, of course I didn't, not fully. And not wanting the opportunity to slip by without addressing my biggest concern, I thought, *So what about Billie-Jean?*

He directed his smile to me. "You really love her, don't you?"

Like a father.

"*Our* Father."

I nodded, making it clear I'd learned the lesson, then asked, *Is she going to be okay?*

He looked back across the room to Stewart.

I pressed in. *She will be, right? I mean that's what I've been praying for.*

He nodded to Stewart, indicating I should listen. I didn't appreciate the diversion but tried my best to obey.

"There is, however, another way to honor his name." Stewart was standing now, underlining his point. "As representatives who actually bear his name, do we accurately represent it? When the jerk cuts us off on the freeway, do I show him the love of Christ? When someone intentionally tramples my rights, or the ones I love?"

The earlier treatment of Chip flickered through my mind. Turning back to Yeshua, I thought, *He's not talking about the kid at the house this morning?*

He continued listening, but I would not be put off. *"She's fourteen. You know what he had in mind.*

"I imagine the same thing she does . . . once she's healed."

She's fourteen. My frustration rose. *Am I just supposed to let him have his way, take advantage of her?"*

"It might have been more in your style than in your content."

My style?

"Shh . . ." He motioned to Stewart who continued.

"We are God's audio-visual aides to the rest of the world. People judge Christ by you. And so, we have yet another way to honor his name. Sometimes we succeed, and sadly, sometimes we fail. Or as the great leader Mahatma Gandhi once said, 'I would be a Christian if it were not for Christians.'"

I sat there, swallowing back my anger, feeling my face grow warm with resentment. Why should I feel guilty when it was the kid who was out of line? Way out of line. When I could stand no more, I turned back to Yeshua to make it clear I did not appreciate his implication, that I was no fan of what he suggested.

But, of course, he'd already disappeared.

Once the service ended, Patricia was quick to usher me out the door and toward her car—but not quick enough. A couple students I recognized from her Bible Club at school spotted us and called, "Hello, Doctor Swenson. Good morning, Doctor."

And me? I managed to get a nod and a Sunday morning smile—which was more than I expected or probably deserved. We continued down the street a few dozen yards to her Volvo. My car was two blocks away—in case anyone recognized it and decided to add a second keying to match the first from last week.

"Listen," I said, "maybe we could grab lunch or something."

"Thank you, Will, but that's not a very good idea." That's Patricia for you. When it came to honesty versus a socially acceptable lie—like having a headache or papers to grade—she opted for the first. Another reason she lacked popularity with her peers. Dishonesty, like any other sin, was something she never got the hang of.

I pressed in. "I was just hoping to hear, you know, more of your thoughts on the sermon."

It was a lie and she knew it.

She pressed the remote to unlock her car. "If you want to discuss Billie-Jean, I'm sorry, Will, but there's nothing more to be said. Your appointment is 11:00 tomorrow at Children's Hospital with Dr. Crispin Martin."

"The pediatric cardiologist."

"One of the best," she said while crossing around to her door.

"And the catheterization?"

"Only if necessary."

"Good morning, Dr. Swenson." A trio of girls passed on the sidewalk.

She gave a nod. "Ladies."

They gave a nod.

She smiled.

They smiled—and continued walking. Not another word was spoken, and yet, somehow, an entire conversation had just occurred.

As they passed and she opened her door, I asked, "How 'bout a quick coffee?"

"Thank you, Will, but no." She quickly climbed inside and shut the door.

I leaned down to the closed window and called, "But we'll keep talking, right?"

She nodded and fumbled with the keys to start the car.

"Day or night," I said. "You've got my number."

Another nod as she worked the gearshift to finally find "Drive."

"Any time!" I called.

If she nodded, I didn't notice as she quickly pulled away—doing everything but leaving a patch of rubber.

"Call me," I shouted. "Any time!"

I watched, a bit puzzled, as she headed down the street. Then I turned to the coffeehouse where a crowd of students had congregated—standing and staring.

CHAPTER
SEVEN

"THERE'S ALWAYS JUNIOR college," Darlene said as she passed me the biscuits. "You're overqualified, but maybe it's best to stay low until things cool down."

"Already tried," I said. "For some reason no one ever gets back to me."

"Imagine that," she said.

"What about high school?" Amber asked. "Or some online continuation thing—you could wear a disguise so no one recognizes you."

"He'd have to learn to turn on the computer," Darlene said.

It was another one of her Sunday dinner productions. This week's costars included Southern fried pork chops, collard greens, buttermilk biscuits, and mashed potatoes with gravy. Boy, could that woman cook. And she took untold delight in educating our "ignorant Northern palates" with what *real food* tastes like. And, between you and me, I believe she also delighted in wearing what must be the most provocative clothes in her closet. Today's wardrobe featured a white, cashmere V-neck that could have used a shirt to fill in a bit of the V.

Though she denied it, I still feared her frequent visits from the mainland were motivated by some sort of romantic interest. She was a good-looking divorcee—a couple times over—who made no attempt to hide the fact she was willing to go three for three, while I, having just been dumped by my ex, was a newbie to the game. Several days earlier, when I had awkwardly tried to explain my concerns and apologize if I'd unintentionally sent wrong signals, I received an angry lecture about overinflated male egos and how her only interest was in befriending poor, motherless Ambrosia. And now, with Billie-Jean in the mix, it seemed Darlene considered herself part of the family. What part I still wasn't clear, which is why whenever she accidentally missed the last ferry and I offered my laundry/office/bedroom to her, I always made a point of mentioning how comfortable I found the sofa.

Speaking of family . . . this afternoon we had a new, though I would make sure, temporary, interloper. Thanks to Amber's and Darlene's insistence, Chip sat across the table from me. I wasn't thrilled about the addition and, despite Yeshua's earlier comments, I was determined to help him move on.

But as I said, the kid was good . . .

"Why even bother teaching?" Chip said while helping himself to a third round of mashed potatoes and gravy. I turned to him as he continued, "Kids don't want to learn that crap. I mean what good is it anyways. Right?"

"Excuse me?"

"I'm serious," he said. "Why should anyone care?"

I threw a look to Darlene who suppressed a smile, choosing to focus on her collards.

"A bunch of dead dudes talking about English country-sides and Grecian pottery?" He shook his head. "Forget it."

Striving to stay civil, I said, "I think you don't fully under—"

"Or moping over some chick who's broken their heart. I mean seriously, talk about a waste of time. This is the twenty-first century. What say we keep it real and talk about what's relevant. Right?"

"And what would you consider relevant?" I asked. "Acting?"

If he heard my irony, he ignored it. "Exactly." He reached for another biscuit. "As an actor I can move people—motivate them, get under their skin."

"I certainly see your point."

Amber shot me a look.

But having found a soapbox, the kid paid no attention. "Change the world, that's what you should do. You still got a few good years left. Right?"

"I'd like to think—"

"So find something useful to do with them, something to fix this train-wreck of a planet you left us."

Sensing my ire, Darlene stepped in. "You don't feel that can be accomplished through great literature and poetry?"

"Like I said, who cares. It's gotta be something for today. Not a bunch of ramblings from a bunch of dead dudes."

I stopped eating. It's hard chewing and gritting your teeth at the same time. After a moment I managed to ask, "And what do you suggest?"

"You're a teacher, so teach. Just don't make it all that boring crap. Try and find some way to be relevant."

That was it. I opened my mouth to unleash all my tenured, PhD wrath upon him when I caught a glimpse of Yeshua standing behind the kid—hands resting on his shoulders. And smiling. At me.

Point made. I didn't like it but got it.

I cleared my throat. "And what, uh, what exactly do you suggest I teach that's, as you say—relevant?"

"I don't know." He flipped his hair. "You're an English dude, so teach English."

"That's precisely what I've been—"

"No, no, no. I mean the language. Like to immigrants, or those migrant worker types that come through here every year? You know, something important."

I took a slow, even breath.

"There *are* night schools," Darlene agreed.

Not appreciating the betrayal, I gave her a look.

"There you go, man. See? Carpus de carum!"

"'Carpus de carum'?"

"Right. Seize the day! Seize the day!"

Darlene returned to the study of her greens.

"What about Billie-Jean?" I motioned to the baby sleeping in her bassinet. "Who'd look after her?"

"Uh, mother here," Amber said.

"I understand. But what if I need to make plans to drive her in for appointments or for treatments?"

"Right," Darlene scoffed.

I turned to her. "What does that mean?"

"Kind of hard to make plans when no one will even give us a clue of what's wrong."

I caught the none-too-veiled indictment and came to Patricia's defense. "Patricia doesn't want to muddy the waters. She knows the cardiologist will give the correct diagnosis."

Darlene shook her head.

"What?" I repeated.

"Would be helpful if Patty stopped being such a tight [insert expletive here] and tell us what *she* thinks."

Amber snorted. "Yeah, what's with that?"

"Makes her feel superior," Darlene said.

Amber gave another snort in agreement.

"C'mon guys," I said. "She's just trying to be professional. She doesn't want to worry us, that's all."

"Good luck with that," Amber said.

Darlene added, "What you see in her is beyond me."

"What I . . .? I don't see anything in her."

"Right," Amber scorned.

Darlene shook her head. "Walking around like she's God Almighty."

"Or the Virgin Mary," Amber added.

The two shared quiet chuckles which only increased my frustration.

Chip didn't help. "Ohhh, she's the one." He flipped back his hair and I looked at him for more. "Miss Stuffy-Butt."

I argued, "She's just trying to help." Darlene scoffed and I turned to her. "Just like you."

"Yeah," she said, reaching for another biscuit, "well I'd keep an eye on her motives if I were you."

"*Her* motives?" the words came from my mouth before I could stop them. "Keep an eye on *her* motives?"

Darlene shot me a look which quickly narrowed into something close to homicide.

Amber and Chip exchanged glances—both having the good sense to keep quiet.

It was a remarkable feat. In one short phrase, I'd managed to destroy the entire meal—reducing the next few minutes into nothing but scraping forks and a cleared throat or two.

When the silence finally broke it was—who else—Chip. "Darlene, you were so right. This is the best meal I think I've ever had." His tactics were obvious, but our only port in a storm. "And you are so right about my Northern tastebuds. Pass the collards." Amber handed him the bowl and he dished them up. "I tell you, I've never tasted anything quite so exquisite." If it got any deeper, I'd have to wear boots. But the derriere kissing seemed to do the trick, slowly inching the conversation toward cordial. Soon we were talking about Darlene's students, Amber's baby and even asking and feigning interest over Chip's upcoming show.

"Yeah," he said, "it's like this contemporary King Lear thing by William Shakespeare. 'Cept we don't follow a script. Seriously, who can understand him anyway. Right? Instead, it's all improv, making contemporary statements upon man's existential existence in an uncaring universe."

"That's so cool," Amber said.

None of us disagreed, at least verbally. Still, despite his lecture and our efforts, the room temperature never returned to normal—even when Darlene served up her killer peach cobbler.

"But no ice cream for you, Pudge Man," she said, dishing out scoops of vanilla for the others. A good-natured though obviously, passive-aggressive barb aimed at the extra weight creeping over my belt. Then there was the fact she couldn't stay and enjoy the dessert with us because of schoolwork—a further sign my forgiveness would come slow and hard-earned.

To underscore the fact, as soon as goodbyes were said and the door shut, Amber turned on me. "Nice, Uncle Will. Real nice."

"What?" I said. Though we all knew what the what was.

"Accusing her of having the hots for you? Really?"

"Senior sex is cool," Chip offered.

"Not now, Junior," I said as I followed Amber into the dining area where Billie-Jean had begun to fuss. "I didn't say that."

"Right."

I held my ground. "Doesn't it seem just a bit odd she spends nearly every weekend here? And the clothes she wears. Believe me, she never dresses like that at school."

Amber scooped up the baby and gently bounced her. "She loves Billie-Jean, alright? And she loves me."

"Love's a beautiful thing."

"Not now, Chip," she said, then turned back to me. "Do you know why she spends all the time around me? Around Billie-Jean?"

"I know why she says."

"Because, she had a daughter once."

I felt my jaw slack.

"Yeah. She didn't tell you?"

I had no answer.

"Of course, she didn't. Cause you're too wrapped up in your own stupid stuff." Looking down to Billie-Jean who continued to fuss, she soothed, "It's okay, baby, it's okay. You hungry? I bet you are. Here you go, sweetie." She pulled up her sweatshirt revealing a bare breast. I looked away, more embarrassed for Chip than myself, until I glanced to him and realized embarrassment was the last thing on his mind.

Amber continued. "She had a kid once. My age, 'cept a few months older."

"Had?" I asked.

"Yeah. And the daughter—she gets pregnant and Darlene insists she get an abortion—she's just a kid, she's got her whole life ahead of her. But the daughter, she doesn't want to get rid of it, but Darlene keeps nagging until she finally gives in. But it's too late and something goes wrong and she starts hemorrhaging on the table."

Fearing the worst, I asked, "And?"

"Daughter and baby both wind up dead."

The room grew still, only Billie-Jean's feeding broke the silence.

"I—I had no idea," I said.

"Yeah. Well, now you do."

CHAPTER
EIGHT

IT WAS 3:40 in the morning and Billie-Jean was crying. No surprise there. Whatever was wrong or wasn't, it didn't change her two to three-hour eating-sleeping-crying cycle. You could set your clock by it—unless that actually involved planning a schedule, in which case all bets were off. After her first few nights at home, Amber and I developed an unspoken competition over who could sleep through the fussing the longest. Winner got to stay in bed. Loser—well that's why I was throwing off the covers, stumbling over Siggy, and shuffling down the hall. Amber was a pro, even with the baby sleeping at her side. They say teens need more sleep than adults and when they crash, they crash hard. Seems a reasonable explanation, except for times like this morning when I scooped up the baby and Amber mumbled, "She needs changing, milk's on the second shelf behind the yogurt next to the cantaloupe."

Still, I treasured these moments, settling into the rocker inside the alcove surrounded by windows overlooking the bay. All was dark and still and silent, except for the soft, diffused moonlight and the muffled lap of water down on the beach.

Hallowed be your name.

I stared at his handiwork in my arms—those tiny fingers, the killer eyelashes, everything miniature, yet complete—so fragile, brimming with possibility. The examination was coming up in just a few hours—and the decision whether or not to undergo a catheterization. *Catheterization*—the very word sounded ominous.

"Dear God," I prayed, "she's so helpless, so vulnerable. Whatever is wrong, make it minor. And please, Lord, no catheterization. Help us. Please—"

"—have mercy on us," a second voice joined mine.

I looked up, scanned the room around me, the beach below. No one was present.

"Lord! Son of David!"

Another voice joined in. "Have mercy on us!"

I glanced down to Billie-Jean. She lay perfectly content with her bottle. Unnerved, but not wanting to disturb her, I carefully rose to my feet and whispered, "Who's there?"

"Have mercy on us!"

I turned around, started into the room. "Where are you? What do you—"

Light exploded around me. I shielded my eyes until I realized I was in bright, noonday sun. As my vision adjusted, I discovered I was walking on a wide, dusty path alongside Yeshua—and about forty or so first-century peasants. Billie-Jean remained in my arms, quietly working her bottle. I pulled the blanket over her head, protecting her from the sun. Behind us rose a city with dozens of palm trees. Ahead, a wasteland of brown, barren hills, and to our right, craggy cliffs.

"Son of David!"

I turned and saw two beggars sitting off the path to our right.

"Have mercy on us!"

"Quiet!" someone from the crowd shouted.

"Mercy! Have mercy on us!"

"Have you no shame?" another shouted. "Don't you know who this is?"

The beggars cried even louder. "Mercy! Son of David, have mercy on us!"

I turned to Yeshua as he slowed to a stop. He acknowledged my presence with a nod.

"Mercy! Son of David! Mercy!"

I leaned into him and whispered, "Persistent, aren't they?"

He quietly answered, "They've been blind a long time." Spotting Billie-Jean in my arms, he broke into a grin. "So this is the little lady."

I pulled back the blanket allowing him to see her face, but the hot sun caused her to begin fussing.

"Shh," he said, "it's okay, little one. Shh . . ." He pulled the blanket back over her face and gently stroked her head.

The crying stopped and immediately turned to quiet coos and a gurgle.

"You've got the touch," I said.

He smiled. "So they say."

"Master, please!" the beggars continued to shout. "Have mercy!"

I motioned to them. "You *are* going to heal them."

"Of course."

"Have mercy upon us! Son of David! Mercy! Mercy!"

"So why are you making them beg?"

"It's their prayer."

I frowned, making it clear I didn't understand. "So why make them beg? If you love them and already know what they want—I know I've asked this before—but what's the purpose?"

He touched my arm. "Hold that thought." He turned to a couple of his men and called, "Bring them to me!"

The two moved into action. Pushing through the crowd, they reached the beggars, yanked them to their feet, and half-pulled, half-carried them toward us. The crowd parted, no doubt expecting the beggars to receive a sharp rebuke. Of course, I knew better. Still, Yeshua avoided my question and as they were dragged toward us I repeated, "Why?"

"There's a deeper love at work here," he said.

"You're going to heal them, though. You said so. And I've read about it."

"You only read about their surface healing. There's something deeper happening in their souls."

The two men arrived and fell to their knees. "Please, Master," they cried, "have mercy, have mercy."

Yeshua looked at them a moment before asking, "What do you want me to do for you?"

"Lord, we want our sight!"

He kneeled to them as the crowd pressed in to watch. Reaching a hand to each of them, he gently rested his fingers on their eyes. They flinched but did not pull away. He silently moved his lips and, after another moment, removed his hands.

Then, rising to his feet, he simply said, "Your faith has healed you."

The men blinked, startled. They looked down to their hands, turned them over, wiggled their fingers. They reached up and felt their eyes. They looked up at the crowd, their faces filled with wonder. They rose to their feet. Several in the group murmured, stepping back in caution. All this as Yeshua watched, smiling in silent amusement. They looked into the sky, down to the ground, every direction they could think of . . . until they started to giggle, then laugh. One even broke into a little dance.

All very impressive, but I was still troubled. As the commotion continued, I leaned back to Yeshua and whispered, "I'm sorry—I still don't understand." He turned to me and I continued. "If you already knew what they wanted, why pretend to be so insensitive by making them beg?"

Turning back to the men, he answered, "Why did I let Jacob wrestle with me all night before I blessed him?"

"In the Old Testament? To be honest, I never understood that."

"My slowness has nothing to do with being insensitive."

"Then—"

"It has everything to do with my love. Its depth."

"By making these guys ask you over and over again?"

He turned to me, a certain sadness in his eyes. "Sometimes that's the only way for you to understand what you *really* want."

I scowled, turning to the men. When I looked back, Yeshua had already started up the road, the crowd beginning to follow. I scrambled to his side.

"You still don't understand, do you?" he said.

"I'm sorry, but no."

He motioned to the beggars who now followed us. "What did they really want?"

"I—" The answer was so obvious I fell silent, suspecting there was more.

He repeated, "What did they really want—more than their sight?"

"I, I don't know. A better life, I suppose."

"And what do you want, Will?"

"I want this baby in my arms to be well! How long are you going to make me ask?"

"Until you hear your real question."

I blew out my breath of frustration. "All right, you tell me. What do I *really* want?"

He shook his head, the sadness returning to his eyes. "That's not my call."

"Not your—" I bit my tongue, knowing better than to respond.

We walked in silence for several moments before he quietly quoted, "'*Your kingdom come.*'"

"What's that got to do with this innocent baby?"

"Keep asking, Will."

"What?!"

"You'll get your answer, the deeper one. Just keep asking . . . and listening."

"I don't understand. Why won't you—"

Suddenly, I was back in the alcove, holding Billie-Jean—standing all alone in the silence and the dark.

CHAPTER
NINE

"ARE YOU OKAY?"

I turned to Darlene. "Me?" I said. "Sure, I'm fine."

"She's just a kid."

"Yeah, no, I get it." I reached for a magazine, one of a dozen on the rack in the doctor's reception area—every cover featuring a happy couple with a happy, healthy baby. I stole a look back to Darlene who still watched me over the top of her own magazine. I smiled, opened mine, and pretended to read.

Ten minutes earlier Amber had insisted Darlene, and not me, be the one to briefly accompany her to the examination room. It hurt a little but by the time Darlene returned I'd pushed it out of my mind.

But Darlene knew better. "You're a good uncle," she said.

I glanced up from my magazine then back down. "Thanks."

"No, I mean it. What you've accomplished with her these past five months has been nothing short of remarkable."

"Well," I cleared my throat, "we've all done our part. I was just one of—"

"Knock it off."

"Pardon me?"

"I'm complimenting you."

"Right, but—"

"Stop being so stubborn and just accept it."

"Accept?"

"That you're a good person."

I shifted in my chair and managed a, "Thanks?" which came off more question than statement.

"You're welcome. See, that wasn't so hard."

I forced a smile.

"And what you said yesterday, about my always coming out to visit . . ."

I lowered my magazine. "Right. Listen, I was way out of line with that. Amber loves your visits and she definitely needs a woman's influ—"

"You were right. I probably do have—mixed motives. And I don't blame you for calling me on it."

"I didn't mean—"

"It's just—you're a good man, Will Thomas." With a shrug, she added, "and good men are hard to fine." She returned to her magazine. "It's important you know, that's all. And accept my apology."

With absolutely no idea how to respond, I settled for a nod and returned to my act of pretend reading.

"By the way, that was my brother on the phone."

I looked up. "Excuse me?"

"When you called Sunday morning? Just so you know." She remained reading. "The fellow you heard when I picked up, that was my brother."

"I—"

"Visiting."

"Right."

"From Yakima."

"I see." Even more confused, I returned to my magazine.

"Just so you know."

I gave another nod, more baffled than ever.

Two hours earlier, Darlene had greeted us at the ferry terminal (at Amber's request). I left my car in the parking lot since her BMW was more comfortable and the chance of making it to Seattle without mechanical failure was greater. I'd been relegated to the back seat with Billie-Jean so the ladies could talk—a position I gratefully accepted since they never seemed to run out of words and, at best, I was good for twenty minutes tops. So, with the sleeping baby in the car seat beside me, I was pretty much left alone to my own thoughts—and prayers.

What did I want? A ridiculous question. I wanted a healthy baby—no complications. And definitely no catheterization. Was that so hard to understand? What did I want? An absurd question. But no less absurd than asking a blind man if he wanted to see? Yeshua said our real needs are deeper than we know. But a healthy baby—what could be more obvious? How could I make someone who claimed to love me so deeply, and who I'd begun to love (yes, I said it) in return, understand? Yes, there were other things, like getting some sort of employment, but Billie-Jean's health, that was the primary issue.

And how did all of this tie in with what I was supposedly learning about the Lord's Prayer?

Granted, he made the *Our Father* part clear, comparing my passion in the hospital with his in the temple. And when it came to *in heaven,* Dr. Stewart's physics lesson on higher dimensions a few weeks back helped. Then there was, *hallowed be your name*—not only through worship, but by being God's audio-visual aide in showing grace to Chip.

So what was next? *Your kingdom come?* That's what Yeshua said to me on the road with the beggars. But what's heaven coming down on earth have to do with Billie-Jean's healing? I shook my head. *What do you want? What do you really want?* The question made no more sense now than it did when he asked it earlier in this morning.

"Mr. and Mrs. Thomas?" The voice jarred me from my thoughts and I looked up to see a sweet, middle-aged nurse. "The doctor would like you to join him."

We both rose as Darlene explained, "We're just friends."

The nurse hesitated.

"*Good* friends," I assured her, hoping Darlene would appreciate the upgrade.

"Like family," Darlene added as we approached the nurse and moved past her through the doorway.

At the far end of the hall was an examination room. We entered it to see Amber sitting on the table, eyes red and puffy, holding Billie-Jean. Dr. Martin, a tall, wizened old man with bushy eyebrows stood beside her.

His voice was raspy, full of gravel. "Mr. and Mrs. Thomas?"

Amber's look pleaded with us to play along.

Darlene and I both answered, "Yes?"

"Would you like to sit?"

"No," I said.

"We're good," Darlene added.

He nodded, cleared his throat, and began—with all the compassion of reading the ingredients on some cereal box. "We have completed all the tests that can be completed at this time. EKG, electrocardiogram, as well as a series of chest X-rays, and, although—"

"What did you find?" I asked.

He cleared his throat over the interruption. "It is too early to say for certain—"

"Here we go again," Darlene muttered in obvious reference to Patricia.

He turned to her and again cleared his throat.

Amber cut to the chase, "Tetralogy of Fallot."

"What?" I asked.

"He thinks it's Tetralogy of Fallot."

I frowned, looking to the doctor.

"Actually," he cleared his throat, "we cannot know for certain. However, signs seem to indicate—Tetralogy of Fallot."

"What is that?"

"As I was explaining to your daughter, it involves four issues."

"Four?" I felt my face growing warm.

"How can it be four?" Darlene asked.

"It is not that unusual. In fact, when it comes to infant congenital heart defects, it is the most common."

My jaw tightened.

"Tetralogy of Fallot, or TOF as we call it, involves a hole in the septum—the wall that separates the two lower chambers."

"A hole in the heart?" I asked.

"Combined with pulmonary stenosis, a thickening of the valve that connects the right ventricle to the pulmonary artery which," he cleared his throat, "carries low level oxygenated blood from the heart to the . . ."

He continued to drone on but I barely heard. *Four! Four defects?* I asked God to fix one and he gives us four!? I looked to Amber who bravely held Billie-Jean. I watched as Darlene moved to her side to comfort her. I turned back to the doctor, trying to understanding the old man's words, but they blurred into rambling nonsense, punctuated by obnoxious throat clearings—as my heart began pounding in my ears louder and louder.

"Will?" I turned and saw Darlene speaking to me. "Are you alright?"

"Mr. Thomas, would you care to sit down?"

I shook my head. "You—you said you can't be certain."

"That is correct."

"So, what . . ." It was my turn to cough. "So should we get a second opinion?"

"A second opinion would be fine. And I can recommend several excellent doctors. But . . ." He let the phrase hang in the air.

"But what?" Darlene demanded.

"Regardless, the child will need a cardiac catheterization."

Catheterization! There it was. The very thing I prayed against? Clearly prayed! Specifically prayed! What game was he playing now? I pushed the thought from my mind, trying to stay in the conversation. "And if—" I tried again.

"If we decide to go through with that procedure, when would you suggest?"

"It is not a matter of *if*, Mr. Thomas. It is a matter of *when*. Check with the nurse but we should have an opening late next week."

"Next week?" Darlene said.

"Correct."

"And if we decide to pass?" I asked.

"I beg your pardon?"

"If we decide to forgo the catheterization?"

"That is not an option, Mr. Thomas."

"And why is that?"

"Catheterization is the only way to determine if we need to go to the next step."

"Next step? And what is that?"

"Open-heart surgery."

PART TWO

CHAPTER
TEN

THE CRAMPED AND windowless room smelled of new paint and old carpet. Two men sat across the table from me. One, an emaciated thirty-something with Coke-bottle glasses. The other, my age, who appeared never to have missed a meal—or any opportunity for a snack. Both wore dark suits, white shirts, and no-nonsense ties.

"Your résumé is very impressive, Professor," the eldest said.

"Thank you."

"And thank you for coming in on such short notice."

"Actually, it was a nice excuse to get out of the house. After Covid it seems the only way people want to interview these days is through Zoom." I wasn't lying. It was a true statement. What I didn't mention was out of seventeen applications, these gentlemen were the only ones who bothered to respond, let alone ask for an interview.

"Yes," the eldest agreed. "Unlike some of the other so-called Christian schools, we prefer to vet our instructors personally. We find it more insightful as to who they really are—their ethics, their code, their morality."

"Absolutely. I couldn't agree more." I silently scolded myself for sounding too eager.

Pushing up glasses that never seemed to stay put, the younger one spoke, his voice thin and nasal. "And, considering your inflammatory comments over televised news, one can only—"

I jumped in. "Yes, I can explain that. It's not what it appears."

The elder nodded. "I'm sure it isn't. Given the media's proclivity toward sensationalism."

I returned his nod, checking myself to make sure it wasn't too vigorous. The two seemed over-starched, even by my standards, but there were those other sixteen applications. I'd heard about this group through Patricia. Their church was starting up a school and looking for an English teacher. I sent an e-mail which wasn't answered and made a follow-up call which they returned within the hour.

It had been eight days since our visit to the heart specialist. We had another three days before the catheterization which I reluctantly agreed to. During that time, I literally had nothing to do except send out résumés, stare at Billie-Jean's pale lips and blue fingers, and demand some explanation from God—who's response was identical to the response of my sixteen applications.

The older gentleman continued, "However, before delving into your unfortunate comments to the media, we have a few questions we'd like to ask regarding your doctrinal views."

My doctrinal views? I wasn't sure I had any. But with nothing to lose, I gave another nod. "Certainly."

Pushing up his glasses, the younger one began. "Do you believe the spiritual gifts mentioned in Acts are still valid for today?"

"Acts?"

"Yes."

I cleared my throat. "To be honest, I haven't gotten that far."

He looked puzzled.

"In the reading, I mean. As I mentioned, I'm still pretty new to all this. But I've started at Genesis and have made it through most of the Gospels, if that helps."

"You do understand, the Bible is not to be read as a novel."

I shot him a smile. "Definitely not a page-turner, is it?"

The two exchanged looks. So much for humor.

Junior pushed up his glasses. "How do you feel about women teaching men?"

"Actually, nearly half the faculty at my university, well, the university where I taught, are women. Though, I suppose we could always have more, you know, to better represent—"

The elder cut me off. "We are not discussing a secular university, Professor. We are addressing the issue of women imparting spiritual truths to men. Within the church."

I looked from one to the other. "Is that a problem?"

"Let me guess," Junior said, "you've not yet studied the Epistles."

"They're on my list."

More traded looks. Things were not going well.

"And same-sex attraction?" Junior asked.

Finally, I had an answer that assured them. "No problem there. I'm definitely attracted to women. That is within the proper boundaries, of course."

The elder took a slow, patient breath.

Junior pressed on. "Do you believe you can be saved even if you're not living in obedience to the Word of God?"

"Well, I try to obey his Word, but sometimes I don't always—"

"Not you personally," the elder interrupted, his frustration appearing more obvious.

"I'm sorry," I said, "I guess I didn't fully understand your—"

"These are rudimentary questions, Professor. You say you're a Christian and yet—"

A familiar voice spoke over him. "Tough crowd."

I turned to see Yeshua leaning on the wall to my right. We had lots to discuss—particularly his refusal to help

Billie-Jean or answer any of my prayers. But that would come later. Right now, I had two future employers to impress.

The elder continued, "—seems that as a college professor, you'd at least be familiar with basic, doctrinal truths."

"How's it going?" Yeshua asked.

I tried ignoring him and barely moved my lips. "I don't understand half of what they're saying."

"Excuse me?" the elder said.

Yeshua shrugged. "Maybe you're lucky."

I frowned.

"Is there something you wish to say?" Junior asked.

"What? No, I just—"

Immediately I was standing beside Yeshua in a wheat field, a breeze gently rippling through it in amber waves. His surrounding men had plucked off some of the heads and were rolling them in their hands, blowing off the chaff. I was not happy at the interruption but before I could respond, a voice shouted:

"You!" I turned to see three men, dressed in robes, standing on the side of a road. "Look what your disciples are doing!"

Picking off his own head of wheat, Yeshua whispered to me, "This should be good."

"They have no right to harvest grain," one of the men shouted, "not on the Sabbath!"

Yeshua's men stopped and turned to him.

He called back to the trio. "Haven't you read what King David and his men did when they were hungry?"

They raised their chins, adjusted their robes.

Yeshua continued. "They entered God's house and ate the sacred bread of his Presence. They broke the law by eating bread intended only for priests."

One of the three started to answer but the oldest held out a hand, motioning for his silence.

Yeshua started through the grain toward them, not angry but determined to make his point. "And haven't you read in the Torah, how the priests broke Sabbath rules by carrying out their duties in the temple on the Sabbath? And yet no one blamed them."

They held their ground, though seemed to huddle just a little closer.

"But I'm telling you, there's someone in front of you even greater than the temple. If you'd only learn the meaning of the phrase: 'I want compassion more than sacrifice,' you wouldn't condemn my disciples. For the Son of Man is Lord over the Sabbath."

Suddenly we were back in the room. The transitions were always a surprise and I closed my eyes a moment to get my bearings. When I opened them, the two men sat staring at me, obviously waiting for an answer. And Yeshua? He sat on their table facing me, casually munching the last of his wheat.

I cleared my voice. "I'm sorry, uh, could you repeat the question?"

"It's quite simple," Junior said.

"Right, um—"

"What are your views of Arminianism versus Calvinism?

"Uh—" I glanced to Yeshua who cocked his head, waiting for my answer.

"Well . . . I'm no historian, but when it came to the Armenian genocide by the Turks in the early nineteen hundreds, there's little doubt—"

"Not the Armenians, Professor. *Arminianism.*"

"Ah, of course. Maybe it would be best for you to first explain the differences as you perceive them? As I mentioned, I'm fairly new to all of this." I threw another glance to Yeshua who offered no help—nothing except the remaining kernels of wheat still in his hand. I gave him a look. He gave me a shrug, then tossed them into his mouth.

"Alright," the elder said, "if that will help."

I nodded. "Thank you."

After a throaty cough, he began. But he'd barely started the lecture before Yeshua broke in. "See how easy it is to slip into what's true instead of the truth?"

"I'm sorry," I said. "What?"

The old man stopped and scowled.

Seeing his expression, I motioned to my ears. "My hearing, it's not what it used to be."

He smiled patiently.

"Think," Yeshua reminded me. "Don't speak. I can hear you just fine without words."

The elder began again. "Arminianism is the belief that once one has committed his life to Christ, he—"

Yeshua leaned back on his hands and spoke, "A perfect example of true versus truth."

Keeping my eyes focused on the old man, I thought, *What's the difference?*

"True is important, but it can overshadow truth.

And truth is?

"Me." Having finished the wheat, he brushed off his hands. "If people aren't careful, their doctrines and dogmas can distract them from my deeper calling."

Which is . . . you?

"Us."

I frowned and he continued. "The deepest calling is for my presence to increase in you until we become one— just as the Father and I are one." He waited. But when no lights came on, he quoted, '*Your kingdom come.*'"

Your prayer.

He nodded. "The kingdom of God is where God is king." He patiently waited for me to catch up. I did my best:

So . . . you're talking about the kingdom of heaven— growing inside me? Coming into me?

"Of course. Did you think I wanted everyone to pray for heaven to drop out of the sky? That'll happen one day, but not yet."

Your kingdom come— I slowly repeated, then added, *Into . . . me?*

"Growing in you and in others, that's right. The kingdom of God is where God is king. It's not just where you go when you die. It's right here and now, inside those who want us to be their king."

I glanced to the older gentleman who kept on droning, "—as opposed to the five-point Calvinist doctrine which contain some of the most—"

Yeshua continued, "These are interesting discussions. But tell me, how do they advance the kingdom of God inside people's hearts?"

I was careful to keep my eyes glued to the older man.

Yeshua pressed on. "Do you remember when we talked about the Tree of the Knowledge of Good and Evil?"

In Genesis, the Garden of Eden.

"That's what's happening here. And back in the wheat field."

But these are the good guys.

"Of course they are. But by focusing on the knowledge of what is good and what is evil instead of me, they've become distracted. They've allowed themselves to be dragged into all sorts of divisions and judgments. If my friends—and they are my friends—would spend less time dissecting doctrine and more time abiding in me, the errors of doctrine would more easily disappear—as naturally as shadows flee from light. As naturally as my love illuminates hearts."

But, I argued, *knowing what's true is important.*

"Not if it overshadows truth."

Which is? He waited for me to answer my own question and I did. *Your kingdom.*

"Good. And when it comes, when it overflows from within and soaks others around you, then—our will is done."

Your kingdom come, I repeated, *your will be done.*

"Exactly. And where is that?" I frowned and he repeated. "Where do we want our kingdom to come and our will be done?"

In us, I ventured. *Here, on earth.*

"Just as it's done . . ." He waited for the obvious answer.

Just as it's done in heaven. He smiled and I couldn't help but repeat my revelation. *Your kingdom come, your will be done—on earth as it is in heaven.*

He broke into a grin. "See, that wasn't so hard, was it?"

I nodded, still marveling at the concept when he hopped off the desk. Patting me on my shoulder he started for the door.

Wait a minute, I turned to him. *Where are you going? I'm still mad at you. We've got lots to talk about.*

"In time."

But . . .

"In time," he said as he passed through the door.

"Professor? . . . Professor?"

I turned back to the men. Their expressions a mixture of concern and irritation. "I'm sorry," I said. "Where were we?"

"I think we have all the information we need for now." The elder smiled. "Thank you for your time."

"Wait, that's it? You don't have anything further to ask?"

The younger pushed up his glasses, "No, I believe you've answered any question we might have."

Realizing what was happening, I tried one last time. "Look, I know I might not be privy to the finer points of these issues, but I'm a quick study."

"Yes," Junior said. "I'm sure you are."

"And I might have come off a little distracted." I threw a quick look back to the door. "But I've got lots on my plate right now."

"We understand." The elder continued his smile. "And we thank you for your time."

I waited.

He kept smiling.

"So, that's it, we're finished?"

"Yes, Professor, I believe we are."

CHAPTER

ELEVEN

ANY SATISFACTION I had understanding that small portion of the Lord's Prayer quickly faded when I realized once again, that none of my prayers had been answered, not even the ones regarding employment. And if my mood was foul on the drive home, it was even worse when I saw Chip's Jeep parked in the driveway. I was angry but not surprised. Our agreement was he'd only visit when I was home which, due to my inability to enforce, was the same as no agreement at all. Nor was I surprised he took my parking spot, leaving me to park up on the road. Before trudging down the driveway to the house, I stopped by the mailbox and pulled out the usual assortment of junk mail—which had easily quadrupled since Amber moved in. Determined to receive her own mail, she signed up on any mailing list she could find.

Once I arrived at the house I opened the back kitchen door and was met by Siggy who showed his usual enthusiasm by chasing his tail into oblivion. Karl, the cat, who couldn't care less, simply sat on the counter—a habit he developed during Amber's pregnancy when she insisted it was unfair for her to bend all the way down to the floor and his feeding bowl.

I dropped the mail onto the counter, picked up Karl, dumping him to the floor, and called, "Amber?" I crossed through the dining area and into the hallway just in time to see the bathroom door close. "Amber?"

"I'm in the bathroom," she yelled.

"I see Chip's car in the driveway." I continued down the hall and paused at her bedroom door which was slightly ajar. Bracing myself for the worst, I pushed it open . . . and there he was, bare-chested, sitting under the covers, pretending to read a book.

He looked up and smiled. "Hey Will, what's up?"

I searched for words.

He saved me the effort. "So how'd the interview go?" He flipped his hair to the side.

Keeping my voice calm and even, I said, "I think you better leave."

"Sure, no problem." He set down the book and threw off the covers. I averted my eyes as he fished for his briefs on the floor. He nodded to the crib squeezed against the back wall. "Billie-Jean's been a sweetheart. You got a real winner there."

"Now," I said.

"Right, right." He found his briefs and slipped them on.

"Take the rest of your clothes and leave. Now."

"Seriously?" He motioned to his shoes, pants, and sweatshirt.

My look was his answer.

"Well, okay then." He gathered his stuff. "You know, it's not what you think."

"Uncle Will!" I turned to see Amber in the hallway. She wore one of Cindy's robes. "We weren't doing anything!"

"It's all good, babe," he said. With arms full of clothes, he slipped past me. "No worries."

"Where you going?" she demanded.

"Your uncle is having a difficult time adjusting."

She turned on me. "It's my life, Uncle Will!"

He paused in the hallway, looking for me to reconsider.

"Go!"

"Alright, alright." He continued down the hall and I followed.

Amber remained at the door and cried out, "Chip!"

"You do know this draconian behavior will only stoke our burning fire for one another."

"Uncle Will!"

He shouted back to her, "I'll call."

"I wouldn't," I said.

"You really can't prevent that," he said.

"Have you heard of statutory rape?"

"That's a thing?"

"It's a thing."

"Chip! Uncle Will!"

We entered the kitchen and he called back, "I love you, Ambrosia!"

She answered, "I love you, Chip!"

He stopped at the door. "I can get dressed here, right?"

I opened the door.

He looked at me, then shook his head and stepped out into the cold. "This is so draconian. It's the twenty-first century, dude." He turned back to me. "You can't just unilaterally—"

I shut the door.

Through the rippled glass I watched as he stood a moment, then turned and with clothes in arm, walked barefoot to the Jeep. Once he was safely on board, I turned back to the hall preparing to meet Amber's wrath. But Siggy added prancing and tap dancing to his tail chasing which meant only one thing. Who knew how long since he'd been let outside. Deciding it best to call a time out before beginning round two, I shouted, "I'm taking the dog for a walk."

No response. No surprise.

"Amber?"

Nothing except an overly dramatic sob—loud enough to be heard from the bedroom, down the hall, across the dining area, and into the kitchen where I stood.

I shoved Karl off the counter—again—and crossed to the door.

"Let's go, Siggy."

TWELVE

"GET 'EM, BOY!"

Siggy needed no encouragement. He'd already bounded across the sand and up the bank after the squirrel. I suppose on good days, I might have tried to call him back. But it's been a while since I'd seen one of those. Good days, I mean. Now everything was mostly about keeping my head above water. And if it meant survival of the fittest, so be it. Was I being vengeful? Of course. Why should some rodent's life be any different than mine? Besides, how many summers have I patiently waited for plums to ripen on the tree beside the house when, just as they were ready, I discovered every one gone, branches stripped bare. And, adding insult to injury, discovering that every fruit was buried in my potted plants—the dirt dug up exposing the roots so they died. No, it was time for the little varmint, no matter how cute, to get a taste of this dog-eat-squirrel world.

I circled the small tidal marsh separating the neighbor's house from mine and pushed through the ferns to join Siggy. He was barking and leaping at the base of old

man Carothers's latest building project—a treehouse overlooking the bay. The grumpy old-timer was scrappy but
could no longer climb ladders, so he'd built a set of make-
shift stairs to his second-childhood getaway. And it was
there, perched atop the landing, the squirrel now sat chat-
tering away and sassing Siggy.

"Go on, boy!" I motioned up the stairs. "Get him!"

But stairs were something new to him.

"Go Siggy!"

He continued going crazy, leaping and barking but
that was it. I suppose it's one thing to scramble up my beach
steps with solid ground on both sides and quite another to
climb a rickety, bare-skeleton version that seemed to float
in midair. But the squirrel would not stop. And neither
would Siggy.

"Go!" I said. "Go!"

But he'd have none of it.

So, I started to climb. "Like this, boy." After the first
couple steps I turned to him. "See how easy it is?"

He didn't.

I climbed several more until I was half-way up and
turned back and kneeled to him. "Come on, boy, you can
do it."

He looked at me, still barking.

I slapped my thigh. "Come on, fella."

He wouldn't budge. It was clear he wanted to join me,
but equally clear he was afraid.

Still, this was one battle I intended to win. So, after a full minute of my coaxing, and a lot more of his barking, he finally took the chance. Keeping his eyes fixed on mine, and with the love and trust only a golden retriever can display, he raised a front paw to the step—then pulled back and resumed barking.

"That's it, boy. You had it. Come on."

He tried again, until the first paw was planted squarely on the step.

"Atta boy! You're doing it. Now the other. Come on."

He obeyed, the second joining the first.

"Atta boy! Come on."

Tail wagging in excitement, he reached for the next step, bringing his back legs up, one at a time, onto the first.

"Atta boy! You're doing great!"

He hesitated as if he were through.

"Come on, Siggy. Come on."

He reached for the next step and succeeded.

"Atta boy."

And the next, and the next, faster and faster, until he reached my side, all squirms and wiggles.

"You did it!"

He resumed barking, this time in celebration. Of course, by now the squirrel had scampered off to another tree but it made little difference to Siggy.

"Good boy, good boy." I let him bask in his success several moments before I finally motioned for us to head back down. "Okay, fella, let's go."

He looked at me, tail still wagging.

"You need to turn around."

The concept seemed foreign—he'd made it this far, why spoil the victory by heading back down?

"Siggy, turn around." I motioned with my hand. "Turn."

He grinned. He wagged his tail. He would not move.

"Siggy."

More grinning.

"Okay then." I carefully dislodged from him and started back down. "You did great, boy. But now you have to come down." I reached the bottom step and motioned him to follow. "Come on, now. Come on."

He refused to budge.

I grew sterner. "Siggy, come down. Now, Siggy, now!"

He stood frozen, watching me, tail still wagging, but this time he added a slight whine.

"Siggy!"

The whining grew more urgent.

I changed my tone. "It's okay, boy, I'm here. Come on down, I'm right here."

He started barking again, but a different type. More of a plea.

"It's okay, it's alright." I climbed back up the stairs, stopping on the step just below him. "I'm right here, fella. You can do this—it's easy, no problem."

He looked at me wagging his tail.

"Just one step, you can do this. I promise."

After more coaxing, he fought against his instincts and finally lowered his head, reaching down for the next step.

"Atta boy!"

But the movement was awkward, leaving his hind quarters above his head. He panicked, lost his balance, and tumbled down the step into my lap, twisting and lunging. I wrapped my arms around him and held tight. "It's okay, boy, I've got you, I've got you." It took several more assurances until he finally trusted me enough to settle down "There, you see. I've got you, you're okay."

Now what? I couldn't carry him, not with my bad back. I tried disengaging, pulling away but he panicked again. "Okay, it's alright."

As he finally quit fighting, I realized my only option. I couldn't lift him, so we settled for a compromise. Still holding him in my arms, I eased my rear to the edge of the step and lowered to the next. It was still clumsy but Siggy felt safe, thumping his tail against me in appreciation.

"There, you see? You can do the rest on your own, right?"

Again, he panicked.

"Alright," I sighed in resignation. "Alright."

I wrapped my arms back around him and, repeating the same procedure, slid down to the next step. He barked and licked my face.

I turned my head. "Okay. I get it, I get it."

And so it continued, one step after another, until we reached the bottom where he felt safe enough to leap from arms and resume barking, throwing in several leaps and twirls in an obvious victory dance.

"Atta boy," I said, rising to my feet. "I'm glad somebody's having a good day."

ço

My dinner that evening, our staple of mac and cheese, was not much better. Amber had barricaded herself in her room, refusing to talk. Not the bonus you'd expect as I was getting used to her chatter. Strange, the peace and solitude I treasured just five months earlier had lost its sheen. Not the peace, but the solitude. More often than not, I found myself enjoying her rabbit-trail-thinking and emotion-ruled logic. Granted, she still had a know-it-all, argue-with-a-blank-billboard attitude, but somehow it wasn't quiet as annoying. And, though I wasn't fond of the constant complaining, I began to understand her outbursts were not so much directed at me, as they were at her own weaknesses and frustrations.

I barely finished the dishes when Patricia called and, as usual, I felt that little spark of excitement.

"Hey, Patricia."

"So how did the job interview go?"

"Not so well, I'm afraid."

"They'd seen the news reports?"

"Actually, we never got that far. We got hung up on all their religious doctrines."

"You say that like it's a bad thing."

"Well, I—"

"Doctrine is needed to hold religion together."

"Right, I just, uh—" I didn't have the strength or knowledge to argue, so I simply left it at, "It just didn't go well."

"I'm sure you'll have other opportunities." That was Patricia for you—sometimes abrupt, but always encouraging.

"Of course," I lied.

"Would you like to come to church with me again tomorrow?"

"Absolutely." The little spark grew brighter.

"Along with Amber and Billie-Jean?"

The little spark sputtered. "I'm afraid that wouldn't be of much interest to Amber, at least for now."

"Pity. Joseph Namaliu, an old family friend from Papua New Guinea, is stopping by."

"Papua New Guinea. That's where—"

"My parents are missionaries, yes. I spoke to him about Billie-Jean and he asked if he could pray over her."

"Pray?"

"For her healing, yes."

I was unsure how to respond. I knew miracles were possible, I'd seen enough of them with Yeshua. But now? In today's world? Still, wasn't a miracle exactly what I'd been praying for?

"He's a wonderful man, Will. Many, many people have been healed by him."

"And he wants to pray for Billie-Jean?"

"Yes. After church at my home."

"Your home?"

"Yes."

"Tomorrow. Sunday."

"Is that a problem?"

"It's just, well Sundays are when Darlene comes over to fix dinner." I quickly added, "And visit with Amber."

"Bring her along."

"Darlene, to church? I don't think—"

She quietly chuckled. "No, no. To my place. We could all meet here in my home."

I paused, thinking it through.

"This is very important, Will."

"Right."

"Wouldn't you prefer sparing Billie-Jean the medical procedures?"

"Of course, but—a miracle?" I frowned. "You're a doctor."

"And a Christian who has seen God perform the miraculous, many times through Joseph. He will only be in town tomorrow. I'm sure Darlene would understand."

"Hmm . . ." I didn't have the heart to explain neither Darlene nor Amber were her fans. And given the fact I was temporarily banned from Amber's life, the chances of convincing her to cancel Darlene for us all to visit Patricia, let alone put her baby in the hands of some faith healer—let's just say I'd have a better opportunity at winning the lotto. Then again, maybe there was another option.

"What if you and your friend came out here?" I asked.

"To the island?"

"Darlene could fix us all a nice dinner and—"

"She would be fine with that?"

"You know Darlene, never one to turn down a party."

There was no response.

"Patricia?"

"I suppose I could check with Joseph. I know he wants to pray over the baby, and if that's the only way."

"I'm afraid it might be—at least for tomorrow."

"Alright. As soon as we hang up, I will call him."

"Great. And I'll double-check with Darlene."

"Good. I can't stress how important this is."

"I understand and I certainly appreciate the opportunity." It wasn't exactly a lie. But not the truth either.

After saying our goodbyes and promising to confirm, I hung up—already feeling I might have made the queen mother of all blunders. Then again, maybe this is what God had in mind all along—*"My ways are not your ways."* Because if it worked, we would have a genuine miracle on our hands and could forego the catheterization. Not only that, but Darlene could see firsthand how God really did exist and cared for our lives. Amber too.

Hmm . . . *Your kingdom come, your will be done.*

THIRTEEN

"I DIDN'T SLEEP with her, you know."

"Pardon me."

"I mean we did, sleep together—but as far as sexual intercourse, she just had a baby. Right? I mean she's pretty sore down there."

"Okay . . ." I'd been showing Chip my rare book collection—Darlene's idea, not mine. To create some sort of bond—Amber's idea, not mine. Truth is, the only reason Amber agreed to meet with Joseph, let alone allow him to pray over the baby, was if I included Chip in the dinner invite. So there I was standing before the glass cabinet, in the nursery Billie-Jean had yet to occupy a single night, showing off my little handful of treasures.

"And this," I carefully pulled out a hardbound, forest green book with gold accents, "is a first edition *Huckleberry Finn*."

He reached for it and I subtly blocked him by opening the cover and flipping to some of the illustrations for him.

"Cool," he said. "How much would you say it's worth?"

"Oh. Well, if you were to put a price on it, I'm guessing close to eight thousand."

He whistled softly. "No wonder you keep them locked away."

I closed the book and carefully returned it to its place.

"Not that I'm opposed to it," he said.

"Opposed to . . ."

"Premarital sex. A couple's physical compatibility is a precursor of what to expect emotionally and intellectually—" throwing me a bone, he added, "and, of course, spiritually."

"Interesting perspective." I reached into the cabinet and pulled out a larger hardback.

Reading the title in my hand, he exclaimed, "*Gone with the Wind*? They made a book of it too?"

"The dust jacket is a bit worn, but it's still in very good condition."

"How much?"

"Maybe six, seven thousand."

"Amazing."

I nodded, pleased we were making some connection.

"So, do you have anything that's not blatantly racist?"

I blinked. "Blatantly—"

"You know, that doesn't denigrate the black experience?"

"Right. I understand, and that's a very good point. However, keep in mind these authors merely reflected the thinking of their time."

"Sure. No, I get it. So, what's it worth? This little library of yours?"

"Monetarily? I'm not sure."

"You've got it insured though, right?"

"Yes, but not everything can be reduced to dollars and cents."

"Will? Chip?" Darlene called, "They're here."

Thirty minutes later, after greetings and some chit-chat, we sat at the table. As usual, Darlene had outdone herself—fried chicken, green beans with bacon, the expected staple of mashed potatoes with gravy, and those incredible buttermilk biscuits. Patricia had offered to help serve, but Darlene had declined. "No, Patty," she said. "Just sit there and be your gorgeous self."

I thought it a compliment but given the exchange of tight smiles, I might have been mistaken.

In the beginning, despite a rather lengthy prayer on Patricia's part, we were all on our best behavior. How often does one have a bona fide miracle worker over for dinner? For his part, Joseph, not much over hundred pounds, was polite, soft-spoken and a bit shy—not at all like the faith healers I'd seen on TV. Still, he was definitely a person of suspect and, although they were temporarily concealed, I knew the guns were loaded.

Nearly ten minutes passed before Darlene fired the first volley. "So, tell us—is it *Reverend*?"

"Actually, it's *Doctor*," Patricia corrected. "He's a professor of Sociology."

"I see," Darlene said. "And for what Bible college is that?"

Joseph's answer was gentle and polite. "The University of Auckland."

"That's in New Zealand," Patricia said. "Auckland."

Darlene smiled. "Yes, I'm glad they haven't moved it."

Unfazed, Patricia replied, "The university is ranked one of the highest in the world."

A faint chill stole over the table as the contestants regrouped, sizing up the competition.

Speaking to Darlene, Joseph said, "Your cooking is very good."

"Thanks. I had to throw it together at the last minute, but it'll do."

Chip flipped his hair and turned to me. "I never asked, how'd that interview go at the church?"

"Not very well," I said. "They seemed focused upon a lot of doctrinal issues which I had no answer for."

"Yeah," he grabbed another biscuit, "all that religious bullsh—" throwing a look to Joseph, he adjusted his language, "—bovine feces." Amber snorted at the humor and Chip smiled in appreciation. "I mean, who needs it, right?"

I glanced to Patricia who pretended to ignore the comment.

"Have you looked into the Department of Corrections?" Darlene asked. "I hear they're always looking for GED instructors."

"Please . . ." Patricia scorned.

Darlene turned to her. "What?"

"Will is so much more qualified than that."

"Excuse me?" Darlene said. "The incarcerated have the same rights as the rest of us."

"Not according to State law," Patricia answered.

Somehow Darlene managed to hold her tongue, though she gave the green beans on her plate a workout.

Chip seized the opportunity to retake the stage. "So tell me, Doctor, do you get to travel around the world much?"

"I am afraid so," he sighed. "Far more than I would like. But there are many who have not yet heard the gospel of Jesus Christ."

"So have you met like any Hindus?"

"Certainly. Several are my friends. Very good people."

"I couldn't agree more. And reincarnation?"

Joseph continued eating. Chip glanced around the table and repeated the question. "What is your opinion on reincarnation?"

Joseph swallowed then answered. "If I were to believe in reincarnation, I would have no need for Jesus Christ to die on the cross for my sins."

"Precisely," Chip said, pleased he'd made his point.

"But, Doctor," Patricia clarified. "You're not saying you agree with the belief."

"What I said is very true."

"But you *do* have a problem with it, yes?"

He smiled. "We have been to church once today. Do you wish to be subjected to yet another sermon?"

"Please," she said. Looking around the table for support. "We'd all like to hear, wouldn't we?"

If anyone objected, we were too polite to voice it. Interpreting our silence—or misinterpreting it—Joseph set down his fork and quietly began. "Several years ago, I visited Nepal." To Chip, he added, "It is a Hindu state."

The kid nodded as if it was a well-known fact.

"At that time, the penalty for discussing Jesus with anyone outside your family was one year imprisonment. If a person were to convert, the penalty was three years. And baptism was, I believe, five."

Darlene was quick to add, "Christians practice their own brand of persecution."

He did not respond, and Chip asked, "What's that got to do with reincarnation?"

"As I traveled the countryside visiting villages, I saw many starving orphans along the road. Several were eating dirt simply to keep their bellies full."

"What about orphanages?" Amber asked. "People to adopt them?"

"It is believed adopting a child would only do them harm. To even offer a drink or some food was frowned upon."

"I don't understand," I said. "What do you mean, 'do them harm'?"

"With reincarnation, if a child's parents are killed, it is believed the child has performed some evil in their past life."

"We call that karma," Chip explained.

Joseph nodded. "So it is considered better for a child to suffer and die to pay for their past sins which enables them to reincarnate to a higher level. If one interferes with karma, then the child's judgment, his suffering, will only extend into his next life."

"That's terrible," Amber said. "What awful people."

He shook his head. "The villagers, good and decent people, simply believe they are acting out of love."

"That's not love," Amber argued.

"In their hearts they believe it is."

"And no one does anything about it?" I asked.

Joseph answered, "We have missionaries there to spread the gospel. But the persecution makes it most difficult. And for many, God's love and forgiveness is a new concept they are not ready to accept."

Darlene quietly scoffed. But no more was said as the table fell back into silent eating.

Round two ended.

But Chip, unable to endure any silence without being the one to fill it, quickly ushered us into the third and final round. "What about your faith-healing business?" he asked. "Is it like a part-time gig? How do people break into that line of work, anyway?"

Joseph smiled. "Trust me, it was not something I pursued."

"I bet," Darlene said to no one in particular.

He continued. "Ever since I was a child, I loved the Bible. I knew Jesus performed many miracles, however I never imagined it would be in our time or that he would use me."

He resumed eating until Patricia prodded him along. "The first time was at my parents' church, was it not?"

"Yes, there had been smaller incidents, but that was the most pronounced."

As he took a sip of water, she explained, "A young couple's baby was sick, actually dead, if I'm not mistaken."

"And . . .?" Amber asked.

Looking up, he saw the expectation on our faces and resumed. "Earlier, I had heard the child was very sick." He looked to Patricia. "Your parents phoned asking if I would come pray for the baby and for the distraught couple. However, I was across town and there was much traffic. By the time I arrived, the room was full of people crying and weeping."

Once again, Patricia clarified, "Because she was dead."

"But this I did not know. I thought the child was merely asleep. I asked the couple if I might hold her. They agreed and placed her in my arms. And immediately she woke up and began to cry."

"What did you do?" I asked. "What did you pray?"

"I did nothing. I was certain I had somehow upset the child and immediately handed her back to the parents with my apology. And the look on their faces—upon everyone's faces . . ." He shook his head, musing. After a moment, he returned to his plate.

"So you brought the kid back to life?" Chip asked.

"I only know she was not breathing and then she was."

"Not breathing for several minutes," Patricia added.

"And that's how you knew you had this gift," Amber asked, "of healing?"

"I don't look upon what I have so much as a gift as merely obeying the will of a loving God."

Darlene had enough. "So if healing is your loving God's will, why is there sickness in the first place? If he has all this love and power, why does he even allow it—pain and suffering? Someone should just call him out and state the obvious: '*Why* God?'"

Joseph continued eating, but Darlene would not be ignored.

"Doctor?"

Looking up, he said, "I think the real question is not, 'Why God,' but rather, 'Why man.'"

Darlene countered, "Man did not create sickness."

His answer was soft, but firm. "For thousands of years we have refused to live by his instruction. We have ravaged his creation, desecrated our very genes."

"Desecrated? How?"

"Through sin."

Darlene scoffed in obvious contempt.

Patricia came to his defense. "According to Scripture, individuals once lived seven, eight, nine hundred years. And today, we've reduced our lifespan to under a hundred."

Darlene turned on her. "Even if that's true, and it's not, if this God of yours is so loving why doesn't he just step in and prevent all this, what you call, *sin*, from happening?"

Joseph nodded in understanding, but it was not enough and Darlene would not be ignored. "It's a simple question, Doctor."

Holding her gaze, he quietly answered, "We are his beloved children, not his robots. What father would program his child only to love and obey him? That is not love. That is slavery. In his great love our Father has chosen to entrust you with freedom. A most powerful gift. How you choose to use it, is up to you."

I raised an eyebrow. Hadn't Yeshua spoken almost those exact words?

Darlene did not back down, refusing to look away. But there was something else in her eyes—the pain of a woman who had lost her daughter. And granddaughter.

And someone who I believe still held herself responsible for their death.

"Right," I broke the silence. "How about some good old American peach cobbler? I've been smelling it the past hour and it's been making me crazy." Turning to Joseph, I explained, "Darlene makes a great peach cobbler."

FOURTEEN

IT WAS ONE of those hot/cold days on the beach. Hot where the clear, bright sun struck; cold in the shadows and biting wind.

"Darlene!" I trotted down the beach after her.

Earlier, when the rest of us had gathered in the living room after dinner, and Amber brought in Billie-Jean—greeted by the appropriate ooh's and ahh's—I noticed Darlene had disappeared.

"Has anybody seen where—"

"Down there." Chip motioned out the windows to where she walked on the beach alone with Siggy. I asked the group to wait a couple minutes for me to get her and they agreed.

"Darlene," I called as I approached. "Are you okay?"

She slowed to a stop and turned. "Me? I'm fine."

"We're about to begin the prayer. You're not going to join us?"

She gave a wistful smile. "You think that's such a good idea?" She pulled aside the strands of hair blowing in her

119

face. "I don't believe that little guy, not for a second. But if there's a chance he can swing something, I don't want to mess it up by bringing in any bad juju."

"You think that's possible?"

She turned to look out over the water. "You tell me."

Unsure how to respond, I changed subjects. "The meal—you really outdid yourself this afternoon."

"I know." She brushed aside more wisps of hair.

"None of this has been easy for you, has it?" I said. "Particularly with that awful experience you had with your uncle, the deacon. And what Amber shared about your—"

"Go, Will."

"Pardon me?"

"Your girlfriend's waiting."

"What? She's not my girlfriend."

Finally, she turned to me—not in anger, but with something in her eyes I couldn't define. "Go," she repeated. "Siggy and I'll be fine."

"But . . . are you sure?"

She looked back out over the bay. "Of course I'm sure. Why wouldn't I be?"

I tried reading what she really meant, but as was so often the case with Darlene Pratford, I was clueless.

"Go."

☙

Holding Billie-Jean in his arms, Joseph turned to me. "Would you pray for us?"

"Me? No, I uh, I don't think—that is to say . . ."

"You are head of the household."

"Yes, but . . ." I turned to the others standing in our small circle—Patricia, Chip, and Amber who remained glued to Joseph's side, keeping a careful eye on her child. "Um—"

"I think he'd prefer someone more familiar with the terminology," Chip said. "Right, Will?"

It galled me, but I agreed.

Joseph looked down at the baby and smiled. "It is not so much the words as it is the heart."

I threw a look to Patricia who came to my rescue. "I think he'd prefer someone with a bit more experience to lead us."

"Yes." I swallowed, grateful. "That's it. Exactly."

Another smile from Joseph. "I understand." He closed his eyes and bowed his head. We took his cue and did the same.

"Father." His voice was soft and quiet. "Our dear Father in heaven. How we adore you, how we honor your holy name." The approach, or formula if you will, sounded identical to Yeshua's. It was a bit stiffer and more formal but still carried a certain intimacy. "We thank you for your tender love and for your great, great power. And we pray, if according to your will, for complete health to be restored to this precious child. We ask this in the authority of your Son, Jesus Christ. Amen."

I stood, waiting for more. Someone coughed. I shifted. Nothing. Eventually I stole a peek. Everyone's eyes were still closed—except Joseph's. He was looking down at the child, grinning and playing with her fingers. I don't know how long we stood like that but eventually, one by one, others opened their eyes, traded glances.

I cleared my throat and Joseph turned to me. "That's it?" I asked.

"Would you like to add something?"

"Well, no, but I mean—that's it?"

Chip weighed in. "What I think Will is saying—we were expecting something a little longer and a bit more dramatic?"

"Do you think that will help?" Joseph asked.

"Well, no. I don't know," Chip said, "you're the expert."

"There are no experts. God hears everyone's prayers."

I could tell the group felt short-changed. All the hoopla for this?

"It's not a matter of quantity," Patricia said. "It's a matter of quality." She looked to Joseph. "Isn't that right?"

He smiled.

She continued, "All we need is to have enough faith." Turning to Amber, she asked, "How are her fingers, her lips?"

Amber carefully examined Billie-Jean then answered, "Still blue."

"Okay—" Patricia took a breath and dug in. "Then we just have to believe a little harder, don't we." She turned to Joseph. "Shall we continue, Doctor?"

"If you'd like."

She nodded. "Yes. All right, then. Let's close our eyes and concentrate harder. And if you should have any doubts, just push them aside, because they have no place here."

As she spoke, Joseph gently passed Billie-Jean back into Amber's grateful arms where she re-examined the baby's fingers and lips.

He closed his eyes and we followed suit. But this time he said nothing.

Finally, Patricia asked, "Doctor?"

I opened my eyes to see him opening his own. He motioned to Patricia, "No, please," he said, "continue."

After a moment's hesitation and a nod of encouragement from Joseph, she closed her eyes and began. "Dear, Jesus. We believe there is nothing you can't do. Nothing whatsoever. And we believe, we *really* believe you can heal this sweet child. And if there are people in this room doubting, we just ask that you forgive them of the sin of unbelief. Please, Jesus. We just ask that you heal this dear child right now." Her voice grew softer, "Please, Jesus—please . . ." until it was barely a whisper. "We believe—yes, we do—help our unbelief . . ."

We stood that way at least a minute, the silence broken only by her quiet murmuring, "Please Jesus . . . Jesus . . ." before she finally concluded, "In your precious and holy name we pray, amen."

Joseph and I quietly repeated, "Amen."

As we opened our eyes Patricia turned to Amber. "How is she now?"

Amber stared down at the baby and answered, a slight trace of anxiety in her voice. "Still the same."

"Are you sure?" Patricia moved to join her. "Look. See, her fingers, aren't they a little less blue? And her lips? Just a little?"

"I don't—" Amber looked harder, "I don't think so."

"Sure, they are."

"Maybe—a little."

"Of course they are." Patricia turned back to us. "We've just got to keep praying and believing. For the baby's sake. If you have doubts, cast them aside. In your mind, picture her healed, because that's how God sees her. That's what he wants. That's what he's promised. We just have to believe a little harder."

The group exchanged looks.

"So, let's try again, okay? Only this time, let's have faith and really believe." Closing her eyes, she began, a bit louder. "Dear Jesus, we really, really believe. We *know* you can do this. And if we have doubts, we ask you to forgive us. Because, 'by your stripes we are healed.' We know this is true. We have faith it's real. So, in your name, we speak healing into this child." Her voice grew more forceful. "Now, Jesus. Now. Be healed! Amen!"

We opened our eyes to Amber, who was already examining the baby—almost urgently—before she sadly shook her head.

"Now, Jesus." Closing her eyes, Patricia raised her face toward the ceiling. "We believe. We have faith you can do it, now. Now, Jesus." She waited a moment and when there was no response, with eyes still closed she said, "Come on, people, we can do this! *He* can do it!"

"Patricia?" Joseph spoke so softly she may not have heard.

"And if you're having trouble, that's alright. Maybe you can step into the other room for a moment. No one will think lesser of you. But without faith the Bible says it's impossible to please God, and this baby really needs—"

"Patricia?"

She turned to him and he silently shook his head.

She frowned. "But you said—you said God wanted you to come heal her."

"No, I said he wanted me to come pray for her."

"But—"

Amber interrupted, the tremor in her voice stronger. "So my baby's not good enough to get healed?"

"No, no," Patricia said, "that's not it. Not at all." She opened her palms and stretched them toward the child.

"Please, Jesus. We know you answer prayer *if* we believe. And we believe, Jesus. We really believe."

I glanced around to the others. No one was joining in.

"Come on, people," she said. "Do we want this child healed or not?"

I looked to Joseph, unable to tell what he was thinking. And to Amber—her eyes brimming with tears.

Patricia continued even more forceful. "Dear Jesus, we believe. We have faith. And we command all sickness to—"

"It's me, isn't it?" Amber croaked.

Patricia stopped and turned to her. "Oh, no, sweetheart."

"Cause of all the crap I've done." She swiped at her eyes.

"That's not true."

"How do you know? You don't know what all I've done." She clutched Billie-Jean tighter and lowered her head so her hair covered her face.

"Sweetheart—" Patricia stood a moment, unsure what to do. "I didn't mean . . ."

Amber choked back a sob.

Patricia reached for her, but Amber turned away, blocking her from the baby.

"I didn't—"

Wiping her face, Amber turned and started for the hallway.

"Amber?" If Patricia thought of going after her, I didn't give her the chance.

"Patricia," I softly said. She turned to me and I added, "That's enough."

"But—" She looked to Joseph than back to me. "We're not believing hard enough. I can feel it. If we just—"

"Enough," I said. "You've done enough."

As she stared at me I saw realization flicker across her face. She looked back down the hall after Amber, then to Joseph, hoping for some encouragement. But Joseph Namaliu, doctor of sociology and part-time miracle worker, simply shook his head, making it clear he agreed with me.

FIFTEEN

I LOOKED UP from my coffee as Darlene, having just come from Amber's room, entered the kitchen. "She going to be okay?" I asked.

"As well as to be expected. I gave her a couple shots of NyQuil PM to put her down."

"You what?"

"You didn't have any booze in the house and I figured you didn't want her scarfing down her little marijuana buttons."

"She has—"

"Welcome to the twenty-first century."

I stepped aside as she crossed to the coffee machine—an addition she'd insisted upon buying—to prevent further martyrdom drinking my instant coffee. "Everyone gone?" she asked.

"Yeah." I watched as she opened the refrigerator and pulled out the French vanilla creamer—another domestic touch I'd grudgingly grown fond of. Finally, more quietly, I added, "Thanks."

"For?"

"You're the only one she'll listen to." I took a breath and blew it out. "I don't know how you do it."

"*Teen Whisperer*," she said as she returned the creamer.

I gave a half smile.

More seriously, she added, "I'm just talking to my younger self." Resting against the counter she continued. "A lot of guilt that kid is carrying around—feeling she's somehow responsible for her sick baby. Then that whole trip your girlfriend laid on her."

"She's not my—"

"Just believe hard enough and everything will work out." She shook her head and swore softly, before taking a sip of coffee.

"You don't buy that?"

"Used to. Long ago and far away. Back when I lived in Never-Never Land."

"Never-Never—?"

"Clap your hands, children, just believe really, really hard and Tinker Bell will come back to life."

"You never resort to prayer?"

"Not if I can help it. And even if I do, it's prayer, not her God-manipulation thing."

I nodded. Like Patricia, Darlene always cut to the chase. She could be a little profane in the process, or what Patricia called, "worldly," but there was also a certain . . . wisdom and groundedness.

She continued, "Remember what Patty's pal said about reincarnation—how its adherents become double victims?"

I nodded.

"Same thing's happened to Amber. She thinks God's punishing her for her sins, and now she thinks he's punishing her for not having enough faith to fix them."

"That's not how it works."

"Tell that to her. And to Patty."

I looked down at my coffee. "Sometimes Patricia lacks certain . . ."

"Social skills?"

"She's a missionary kid, remember? Grew up in the jungles."

"I've got nothing against her, Will. Really. Though she can be a little judgy."

"She's got strong principles, I'll give you that. But I've never heard her judge anyone."

"I'm not talking about judging others. I'm talking about judging herself. The woman is relentless."

"She pushes herself pretty hard."

"And that self-judgement, whether she wants to or not, just winds up spilling all over the rest of us."

I thought a moment then slowly nodded. It was true. Not once did I recall Patricia judging someone, and yet I always felt guilty around her, like I never quite measured up—which made Yeshua's statement about me helping her, instead of the other way around, all the more confusing.

"Seriously," Darlene said, "it's hard to believe you two even have the same God."

I frowned. "What do you mean?"

"She's all about her faith and religion, while you . . ."

"While I what?"

"Underneath all that cynicism you pretend to have, you can really be a sensitive guy. Sometimes too much."

"Must be the artist in me."

"Or the crybaby."

Touché.

"And these last few months, the changes I've seen." She hesitated, then continued. "Maybe it's just having Amber around, but it's like you've finally found your center. Don't get me wrong, you're still a piece of work, but, there's something . . . different."

"Must be all that prayer."

"Jerk."

I smiled and took another sip of coffee. "So, you spending the night?"

"If you don't mind."

"The sofa and I are getting to be old friends."

"You don't have to sleep out there you know."

I gave her a look.

She shrugged. "Can't fault a girl for trying."

I glanced back down to my coffee. It wasn't the first time she'd made the invitation. Like I said, she had no problem speaking her mind. And though we both treated the offers lightly, they were becoming harder to ignore. At least for me. Especially on those lonely nights when I'm staring up at the ceiling unable to sleep. Or the rainy afternoons when I'd love to share the latest bit of poetry I've discovered, or piece of literature, or even some of my clumsy attempts at writing. And yes, I found her attractive. Not in the drop-dead, cover girl way of Patricia—but as someone closer to my age, more assured, and whose sharp angles of youth had gradually given way to something softer, more relaxed. As with her personality, Darlene was at ease in a body she had grown comfortable with.

"On second thought . . ." She finished her coffee and set the mug on the counter. "If I hurry, I can catch the last ferry out."

CHAPTER
SIXTEEN

YOUR ARM'S TOO Short to Box with God. It was the title to a musical I saw long ago and forgot—until recently. Go figure. I know I have a tendency to shut down and cut people off over disagreements—one of Cindy's hundred-plus reasons for leaving. But I'd been getting better; at least toward Yeshua. Sure, there were still times I pouted and sulked, but they seemed to come less frequently—I hoped. Not that I understood what he was doing, but somewhere in the back of my mind, I knew it was always for the good, always out of love. Confusing, but out of love. That's why, the following morning, a few hours before we took Billie-Jean in for the catheterization, I read with some satisfaction, the following verses from Isaiah:

> *"For my thoughts are not your thoughts, neither are your ways my ways," declares the* Lord.
> *"As the heavens are higher than the earth, so are my ways higher than your ways and my thoughts than your thoughts.*

> *"As the rain and the snow come down from heaven,*
> *and do not return to it without watering the earth*
> *and making it bud and flourish, so that it yields seed*
> *for the sower and bread for the eater, so is my word*
> *that goes out from my mouth: It will not return to me*
> *empty, but will accomplish what I desire and achieve*
> *the purpose for which I sent it."*

I sat in the alcove during the early light of dawn, mulling this over when, suddenly, a bird crashed into one of the windows. Not from the outside, but from inside. I'd left the kitchen door open just wide enough for Siggy to go out and do his business—and just wide enough for a sparrow to fly in.

And he didn't just hit the glass once. He banged into it over and over again, relentlessly trying to get out. As far as he was concerned, freedom was right there in front of him. I rose to my feet, ran back to the door to open it wider, then returned, waving my arms, trying to direct him toward it. But he continued to slam into the glass, causing me to cringe with every thud.

Thinking I could somehow catch him, I raced to my laundry/bedroom/office and grabbed a blanket. When I returned, there were a dozen smudges on the glass. Some bloody. And still, he wouldn't stop. Who could blame him when the sky and ocean were right there in front of him? I inched forward and when he was within range I threw the blanket to cover him. I missed and only grazed him, causing him to panic even more. I tried again. And failed again. Third time was the charm. The blanket covered him and he fell to the floor. Dropping to my knees, I quickly gathered the edges and trapped him. As I rose and carried him across the living room and to the kitchen door, I could feel his little body fluttering and flapping against the material. Once outside, I opened the blanket and watched him dart out and away.

"Nicely done," a familiar voice said.

I looked to see Yeshua standing near the doorway. "Thanks," I answered, then turned back to try and spot where the bird had flown.

"Pretty confused, wasn't he?"

"He didn't understand why he couldn't get out. That I was only helping when . . ." I slowed to a stop then turned back to Yeshua. There was no missing that familiar twinkle in his eyes. "Let me guess," I said. "Another metaphor?"

He grinned. "Everything's a metaphor."

I gave the blanket a shake and headed back inside. '*My ways are not your ways*,' I quoted.

He followed me into the kitchen. "See. You really are getting it."

"Coffee?" I asked.

He shook his head.

"Still not a fan?"

"Water's good."

I nodded and pulled a glass from the cupboard. "Can I ask you a question—about yesterday's prayer."

"Just one?"

I turned on the tap and filled the glass. "You say you always answer prayer, right?" I handed it to him and watched as he took a long, satisfying drink.

"Thirsty?"

He finished and looked at the empty glass, marveling with a sigh. "Still one of my favorite creations."

"About prayer. You say all we need is faith. And yet, Patricia had it and you did nothing—except put her on the spot."

"Actually, she put herself on the spot."

"Darlene called it, *God manipulation*."

"Not a bad description."

"But what about faith?"

"Absolutely necessary."

"She had it. More than all the rest of us."

He shook his head.

"Then how much does it take?"

"Just a mustard seed."

I scowled, not understanding.

"She had plenty of faith, Will. Just the wrong kind." Seeing my expression, he went on to explain. "She had faith in her faith. Not faith in us. She believed we would heal Billie-Jean and that's a good start—but she didn't believe enough to let us do it our way."

"'*Your will be done*'?" I quoted.

"On earth as it is in heaven." He handed me the empty glass, motioning for more.

I began refilling it. "You see, that's what's so confusing. Why bother praying if you're just going to do it your way?"

"We are and we're not."

"I'm sorry?"

"Your faith is the catalyst; it sets our power into motion. Remember how much we enjoy those Father/Son projects?"

"Right . . ."

"Your job is to pray, not tell us how to do it. That's our job."

"To make it happen."

He nodded. "You pray. We do."

"But only if it's *your* way, your will." I handed him the glass.

"Would you have it any different?"

I wasn't sure how to answer.

"We're your safety net. Our will stops you from doing stupid things." He took another long swallow.

"And yet—we still have free will, right?"

"To do stupid? Absolutely."

I leaned against the counter, thinking.

"Do you remember reading how the Israelites insisted on being ruled by kings instead of our prophets? 'Everybody else has a king,' they complained. And, boy, could they carry on—whining and begging and sulking."

"And?"

"We eventually let them have their way—with all the accompanying problems." He set the glass on the counter. "Faith, it's not some mind game, Will. It's not forcing yourself to believe something to make us perform. Faith is learning our will—then speaking it into existence."

"And I learn your will by . . .?"

"The same as with anyone. By getting to know us. Hanging out with us. Learning how we think."

"So we're back to what you call . . . *abiding*."

Suddenly I was all alone in a shaft of moonlight. I stood on the edge of some worn, dirt path. It dipped into a small ravine to my right then moved up a hill. To my left, it entered a gate in a tall wall. Inside I could see lamps and small fires flickering—along with Yeshua and his group of men emerging. Even in the shadows, there was no missing the fatigue and sadness filling their faces.

Yeshua was speaking as they approached. "Remain in me as I remain in you. No branch can bear fruit by itself; it has to stay attached to the vine. The same goes for you. You can't bear fruit unless you remain in me."

I stepped aside to let them pass. If he saw me, he gave no indication.

"I am the vine," he said. "You are the branches. If you remain in me and I in you, you will bear plenty of fruit. But apart from me you can do nothing."

He spotted a large stick not far from my feet—a dead olive branch, the best I could tell—and stooped to pick it up. "If you choose not to remain in me, you'll be like this branch," he turned it over in his hands, "all withered and good for nothing—except firewood." He tossed it to the side of the path and turned—this time directly connecting his eyes with mine. "But if you remain in me and my words remain in you, ask me *whatever* you want, and it will be done for you."

I felt my cellphone buzz and pulled it from my pocket. As I did, his voice began to fade. "This is for my Father's glory, that you bear much fruit . . ."

I checked the ID, saw it was from Dr. Martin.

". . . showing yourselves to be my disciples."

I cupped my hand around the phone and whispered, "Hello?"

"As the Father has loved me, so I have loved . . ."

"Mr. Thomas?" a woman's voice asked.

"Yes."

"This is Dr. Martin's office. I'm afraid there's been an emergency."

I stiffened and suddenly found myself back in the kitchen. All trace of Yeshua and the men was gone. "An emergency?"

"Yes, with another patient."

I felt myself relax.

"We'll have to reschedule the catheterization, postpone it until Tuesday."

"Tuesday?" There was no missing the concern in my voice. "That's four days from now."

"Yes. The doctor says it should be no problem."

"Maybe not for him."

"If you'd like, we can recommend you to another specialist."

"And wait, what, another two weeks?" There was no answer. "Alright, fine."

"How does 3:30 sound?"

"You don't have anything earlier?"

"Not until the end of the week. We could schedule you for—"

"Three-thirty will be fine."

"Alright, then. 3:30 Tuesday. And if you have any questions, don't hesitate to call."

Of course, I had questions. Like what type of emergency did they have? Was it another catheterization? If so, what went wrong? Could it go wrong again? Instead, I settled for giving a curt goodbye and hung up. I stood a moment, fuming—until my eyes fell upon his empty glass setting on the counter. I shook my head, muttering an oath, as I turned my back on it and walked away.

PART THREE

CHAPTER
SEVENTEEN

"THAT'S IT?" I asked. "You have no more questions?"

"No, not really. Your résumé is stellar. The very fact you would apply here is, well it's quite a plus for us."

"You've seen the news reports?" I asked.

The man on Zoom—graying buzz-cut, sharp, angular features—nodded. "You made every channel."

"It was taken out of context," I said, "but I'm curious why you don't see it as—"

"A problem? To be frank, Professor, it may help you better connect with the men here. Particularly those in the Cedar Peaks Unit."

"Cedar Peaks?"

"Where we house the sex offenders."

"I was quoted out of context."

"A fact that may or may not be lost on them."

I paused, wondering what I'd gotten into. Still, some employment was better than no employment—which at the moment was my only other option. And with Billie-Jean's procedure coming up in two days along with the previous medical bills from her unconventional birth, the *Titanic* had better chances of staying afloat. So, with no other game in town, I took Darlene up on her suggestion and started contacting the prisons. This one in Snohomish was last on my list and the only one to respond.

"Will I be—" I cleared my throat, "safe?"

"Of course. If you want, some of the classes can be online."

I shifted, double-checking the screen to make sure the diplomas were visible on my office wall, while simultaneously making sure the washer and dryer were out of sight.

"So when do you think you can start?"

"I, uh, I would need time to prepare."

"I'm not sure how much of that is necessary, Professor. Granted, some of the men are serious about continuing their education, but most are just bored or want it on their record come parole time."

"Nevertheless, I should check GED protocols and requirements."

"Is next week too soon?"

"We have a few family medical issues to clear up." Then, at the risk of jeopardizing the opportunity, I quickly added, "How about the first of the following week?"

"We'll take what we can get." (Funny, I thought, that should have been *my* line.) He continued, "In the meantime, we'll be sending out some paper work and running background checks. Strictly routine."

"I understand."

"Okay then. Let's reconnect the first part of next week."

"That would be terrific. Thank you."

"No. Thank you, Professor."

And on that ominous note, we ended the call.

"That went well."

I turned to see Yeshua sitting on the washer in his white robe and sandals like everything was fine. For a moment I thought of ignoring him, teaching him a lesson—but it's hard ignoring God the Son when he's sitting on your washing machine.

"They seemed a little eager," he said.

I glanced at the screen. "More like desperate."

"And for good reason." I turned to him and he continued. "Why would someone with your credentials want to teach a bunch of low-life losers?"

I frowned at the comment then saw the glint of mischief in his eyes. Realizing his point, I said, "So you don't agree with Patricia? You don't think I'm wasting my time and talent?"

"Not unless you think *I* am."

My frown deepened.

He answered, "Give up my place in heaven to come down and hang out with you."

"That's . . . different."

He titled his head at me quizzically. "How so?"

I started to give an answer then realized I had none. Reaching over and shutting down my computer, I said, "I suppose it's better than nothing."

"Give us this day our daily bread."

"Believe me," I sighed, "with the money they're offering, bread's about all I'll be eating. They can't even promise me full-time. Talk about slim pickings."

"Actually, that depends upon the bread."

Before I could respond, we were standing in the back of a small, first-century room—dimly lit, roughly plastered walls, stone floor. I was about to say, "Now what?" When I recognized the men sitting on the floor—his disciples. Their faces flickered in the light from a couple oil lamps resting on a low-lying table they'd gathered around. At the center, sat another Yeshua. I turned to the one standing beside me. He was intently watching the men pass around a cup—each raising it to their lips and taking a solemn drink from it. Everyone was deathly still.

I leaned to Yeshua and whispered, "Is this the Last Supper?"

He continued watching in silence. The moment was too important for me to interrupt.

As the cup finished its rounds, Yeshua at the table raised a piece of flat bread into the air with both hands and spoke—his voice soft, filled with passion. "This is my body which is given to you." He tore the bread in half. And, in the silence, handed the pieces to the men on either side. "Eat this in remembrance of me."

Sensing the importance, each man took it and tore off a piece then handed the remainder to his neighbor.

Trying to make the connection to our conversation, I whispered, mostly to myself. "Bread."

Yeshua beside me nodded. "I am the bread of life." I understood, but he had a further point to make and turned to me. "Your *daily* bread."

"Daily bread?"

He focused back on the scene and continued quietly, "So many feed upon me only once a week. They would never do that with their bodies. They stuff their stomachs but starve their souls."

I turned back to the scene and softly repeated, "Give us this day our daily bread."

He nodded. We continued watching in silence as the bread made its rounds until it reached the man I'd come to recognize as Judas. He hesitated then looked to Yeshua at the table. Yeshua gave him a silent nod; so slight it's doubtful anyone saw.

Judas took his cue and ripped off a piece as I quietly marveled, "You were still reaching out to him, even then."

"'*Forgive us our debts,*'" he quietly repeated, "'*as we forgive our debtors.*'"

"Even as he's betraying you?"

His voice thickened. "My love never stops." Turning to me he added, "In time, neither will yours."

"Love my enemies," I said.

"You have no enemies, Will. Only opportunities."

I scowled. "Even *you* had enemies."

He shook his head. "In the new contract there are no enemies—only prisoners of war."

I held his look, slowly digesting the thought. When I turned back to Judas he was quietly chewing, his face a conflict of emotions. "'*Forgive us our debts*,'" I repeated, "'*as we forgive our debtors*.'"

The scene flickered until we were back in the laundry room.

I turned to Yeshua who still sat on the washer. "But I've done that part, right?" I said. "Forgiven his debts? My old man, I've forgiven him."

Yeshua mused, "You still have a couple more *opportunities*."

I didn't have to think hard before Chip came to mind. And if I thought it, I knew Yeshua heard it. "The kid's a con artist," I said. "From the word go. And he's just using Amber; you know that."

He said nothing.

"Hey," I argued, "at least I'm trying."

He smiled. "Which is one of the million things we love about you. You have a long way to go, Will Thomas, but you're always trying—and everyone's cheering you on."

"*Long way to go?* So, I still have to—" I pushed the thought of dealing with Chip out of my mind. "Who else?" I asked. "Is there anybody else?"

He looked at me.

"You said a couple. I have a 'couple more opportunities.' Who else is there?"

He took a long, slow breath.

"Who?"

Finally, he answered. "Just me. You have to forgive me."

"*What?* After all you've done for me, up on that cross? How can you say that?"

He smiled though there was a hint of sadness about his eyes.

"Okay," I admitted, "you get under my skin a little, but—"

The smile grew.

"Alright, sometimes a lot. I mean things would be a lot easier if you answered a few prayers once in a while—or at least filled me in on what you're doing."

"My ways are not your ways."

I sighed. "I'd just like to get on base once in a while; score a point now and then."

"You're not in it to score a point."

"I know, I know. You want me to win the whole flippin' game."

He looked down and chuckled.

"What?"

"You're not winning a game, Will. You're heading for the Hall of Fame."

I felt my jaw slack, then scoffed and shook my head. As was often the case, he thought way more of me than he should. I changed subjects, back to something more comfortable. Motioning to the computer, I asked, "So you think I should take this job then? Even though it's part-time?"

"Part-time will let you pursue your real passion."

"My real passion is to teach."

He gave another chuckle and before I could respond, we were interrupted by the crunch of gravel in the driveway. I stood up, pulled back the curtain, and saw Chip's yellow Jeep pulling in. "Seriously?" I said. "Now?" When there was no answer, I turned. But, of course, Yeshua was gone.

EIGHTEEN

DON'T ASK ME how (though I have a pretty good idea of *who*), three and a half hours later I sat on a folding metal chair with Amber and Billie-Jean between us in a tiny "theater" that smelled of dust, new wood, and mildewing carpet. Up on stage—a newly constructed platform, five by ten feet, Chip and his fellow thespian, a premature balding and barely bearded Dylan somebody-or-other, were in the midst of their first (and if there's a merciful God in heaven) last improv performance.

"Women," Dylan sighed with all the wisdom of someone just out of puberty, "don't get me started."

"Yeah," Chip quipped, "but they sure get *me* started. *Vroom, vroom, vroom . . .*"

"You got that right," Dylan chuckled. "But seriously, one minute they want sex, the next they don't."

"I hear that."

"Why can't they just be groveling dogs like us?"

Chip tilted back his head and howled.

Dylan patted him on the head. "Easy, big fella, easy." To which Chip rapidly tapped his foot like a dog enjoying a good scratch.

It was a special presentation for select patrons (there were four of us, five if you count Billie-Jean) in an effort to raise funds for their upcoming production of *King Lear*. Earlier, I tried to talk my way out of it, offering to stay home with Billie-Jean, but since my patron possibilities were greater than Amber's and since Yeshua's lecture on forgiveness was still ringing in my ears, well . . .

"And commitment." Dylan threw up his hands in frustration.

"Yeah, what's with that?"

"A movie, a dinner—"

"An expensive one if she's hot."

"Exactly. I mean what more do they want?"

"Not as much as we do, if you know what I mean."

"You got that right, bro." They high-fived.

I snuck a peek at my watch, wondering if military intelligence knew the effectiveness of this type of torture. As an old-schooler, I didn't appreciate the sex talk, though I did feel a certain bond in their inability to understand women. And Amber? She was absolutely mesmerized. True love. Not only is it blind, it's a pretty poor judge of entertainment.

But Dylan was on a roll. "I look at dating like a buffet. I mean who wants to limit themselves to just one selection.

Some days I may want Asian, other times Mexican or Italian, you know what I mean?"

"Yeah, bro, I get it. Except all that fancy eating can give a guy indigestion."

"Not if you stay away from Mexican."

I cringed as they laughed and knuckle-bumped. Knowingly or unknowingly, they'd just managed to sound both sexist and racist. If insensitivity was the mark of a true professional, they were both on their way to the big time.

"What I'm saying," Chip continued, "is if you find the right girl, maybe one is all you need."

"What? Are you feeling okay?"

"I'm serious, dude."

"Not a Covid relapse?" Dylan said. "No fever? No headache?"

"Nah. Just a major case of *heart burn*."

"Heart burn? Over some chick?"

"Yeah." Chip shook his head. "It's like she's all I can think about, know what I mean? Sometimes I can't even go to sleep at night."

I stole another look to Amber who was leaning forward, drinking in every word.

"Wow, dude, you got it bad." Dylan suddenly stepped back.

"What are you doing?"

"Social distancing." He turned to the audience, "Anybody got a facemask?" Then back to Chip, "Let's hope there's a vaccine."

"I don't know, dude. If there is, I don't think I'd take it."

"You're serious."

"Yeah." Chip looked straight out at Amber. "And I hope I never recover."

I winced at the bad acting. Either that, or he really was some love-struck kid bearing his soul. Amber's dreamy sigh said she bought the later. Even Billie-Jean gave a little gurgle.

Unbelievable.

Thirty minutes later we were invited to the "lobby" for a meet-and-greet with the cast.

"So, what'd you think?" Chip asked.

"You were wonderful," Amber said.

"Really?"

"Really."

"No, I mean seriously."

She took his hand. "I'm so proud of you."

Amazing. The kid actually glowed. If he'd dished it out on stage, Amber was now returning the favor. Either that or— No, the look on both of their faces was real. Over-the-top but real. And as I stared I could feel faint memories stirring. That time, so long ago, when I, too, couldn't sleep. When, after Cindy agreed over the phone to our second date, I burst out of my apartment door, running down the street shouting, "She said yes! She said yes!" Followed by all those months of knowing I'd slay any dragon for her, spend my last dollar, do anything to make her happy.

When did that dry up, evaporate? When did that reckless joy—the drunken giving, giving, and more giving—turn into power plays and keeping score?

Maybe it was time for me to back off. A little. I didn't have to like Chip—a big amen on that—but I could at least give him the benefit of the doubt. Maybe it was time to loosen up, relax my grip, and enjoy watching the emotional insanity of two youngsters so high on love they'd risk everything for each other. Maybe everyone deserves that experience at least once in their lives.

Dylan, on the other hand . . . . I tried my best to be civil as he shared the trials and tribulations of starting a new theater company. And I almost pulled it off—until he unfolded the donation check I'd just written and read: "Twenty dollars! That's great, man. Now I can finally buy the cast a cup of coffee. He laughed and I managed a polite chuckle. It was only when he held the check up to the light saying, "Looks like you got room to squeeze in a couple more zeros," that I chose to quit trying.

Later, as Chip, Amber, and I sloshed through the muddy gravel to our cars, I bit the bullet and asked Chip if he'd like to join us for dinner. "Nothing fancy," I said, "just some place to, you know, chew the fat."

Amber made a face. "We're both vegan, why would we want to chew—"

"No, no," I laughed. "That's just a colloquialism for talking."

"Kind of a gross one," she said.

"Actually," Chip said as we arrived at the cars, "me and Am, we were planning to grab something on our own. You know, talk stuff over. *Chew the carrot*," he laughed.

I smiled. At least he was trying.

"And with Billie-Jean," Amber said, "so you don't have to babysit or anything."

"Sounds good." I turned to unlock my car. "Just try to be home before 10:00."

"Sure," Chip said. "No problem."

But as I opened my door, I spotted the car seat in back. "Hang on," I said, "you'll need this."

"We're good," Chip said as he opened Amber's door.

"No, it's the law," I said. "To keep Billie-Jean safe, you need a . . ." I dropped off as his cab light came on revealing a baby car seat strapped in back.

"You bought a car seat?" I asked.

"Sure," he said as he opened the back door and sat Billie-Jean down in the seat.

"But—those things, they're expensive."

"Sure are." Chip grinned. "But worth every dime." He flipped his hair to the side. "Right?"

I nodded, watching as he worked the straps and buckles. Then, almost against my will, I found myself walking over to Amber, pulling out my wallet, and handing over a twenty.

She took it without comment or thank you.

CHAPTER

NINETEEN

THIS TIME WE drove two cars down to Seattle—Darlene's and mine. Not because we were excited to spend the extra money on gas but to give Amber and Darlene some extra girl time. Actually, some non-Uncle-Will time. I'm not sure how I constantly wound up being the bad guy, but everybody has a role. Typecasting, I suppose.

Patricia had classes to teach, but the day before promised to devote the next twenty-four hours to prayer and fasting. I wasn't sure how many meals that bird skeleton of hers could stand missing, but she was definitely determined and I thanked her. I also began wondering if that was the missing ingredient in my unanswered prayer. Folks certainly did enough fasting in the Bible. So . . .

I managed to make it through missing yesterday's breakfast and lunch. No problem. It wasn't until midafternoon things got uncomfortable. Not only for me, but for Siggy, Karl the cat, and any other object, live or inanimate, that got in my way—ice cube trays put back empty, my last inch of medicine cabinet space overrun with yet more baby paraphernalia, Amber's socks left wrong-side-out in the laundry. You name it, I was cranky over it. Low blood sugar and I are not pals.

But I wasn't content to just fast. I'd spent half of yesterday poring over the Bible looking for other ways to twist God's arm. Yeshua could talk all he wanted about the Lord's Prayer, but I needed more than talk. If I was going to convince God to get off the dime and put him into a full court press, I was going to use every tool in my toolbox. (And, yes, I realize I've just mixed three metaphors in one sentence, but you try going twenty-four hours without eating.)

If it meant walking around the house seven times and praying like they did at Jericho, I'd walk around the house seven times and pray—despite Amber's eye rolls, oh, she of little faith. If it meant lying prostrate on the laundry room floor, I'd lie prostrate on the floor (with door shut and locked). I will admit I might have gotten a little carried away when it came to visiting the local hardware store to check out shovels.

"Got anything sturdier than this?" I asked the young clerk as I weighed the heaviest of the choices in my hands.

"No sir. That blade is top of the line."

"I'm not talking about the blade; I'm talking about the handle."

"Um . . ."

"Never mind. I'll buy two."

"O . . . kay . . ." The kid was careful not to ask any more questions. He recognized I was the same madman who weeks earlier raced out of the store with a crowbar, sledge hammer, and other assorted tools to help deliver a baby.

The point is, I'd read of some Old Testament king who was ordered by some Old Testament prophet to hit the ground with a handful of arrows. He obeyed, but only a few times and was scolded for his half-hearted faith. As a result, he received only a portion of what he could have. Well, that sure wasn't going to be me. If beating the ground was necessary to get God's attention, I'd beat the ground. The harder the better—resulting in one broken shovel handle, one purchased replacement, and one backup just in case. Like those blind men on side of the road, I wasn't giving up.

Now, just past 3:30 in the afternoon, we pulled up to a small office building north of the University of Washington. We entered the suite which, despite having no windows, did its best to feel homey and comfy—overstuffed chairs, throw pillows, and cheery wallpaper with the occasional Photoshopped mountain stream. A sweet, grandmotherly receptionist fit right in. "Well, hi there," she said, "you must be the Thomas family." We nodded, all complicit. "And you must be Billie-Jean," she said. "Aren't you just the sweetest thing? The doctor will be out in just a few minutes to go over the procedure. In the meantime," she handed me a clipboard with half a dozen printed pages, "here's some paperwork for you to fill out. Got to love that paperwork, right Grandpa?"

I caught Amber giving another eye roll.

We took our seats and I went to work on the forms. They were similar to the last round at the previous office except for the additional final page labeled, "Acknowledgment of Risks." There were plenty of fine-print details, but the phrase catching my attention was:

". . . in the unlikely event of allergic reaction to medicines or contrast material, as well as possible stroke, heart attack, or kidney damage."

"Yeshua," I whispered, "what are you doing?"

Of course, there was no answer.

Clenching my jaw, I signed just as Dr. Martin, his eyebrows as shaggy and unkempt as ever, appeared. After greeting us, he sat and prepared to explain the procedure.

But he barely had time to cough away the phlegm before Amber interrupted. "We read it on the internet."

He smiled. "I'm sure you have but let me go over a few things to put your minds at ease." Although he was the same man as before, his speech was less official and kinder as if he'd just taken a Berlitz course in Bedsideese. Clearing his throat, he continued. "First, we will give Billie-Jean a sedative so she can have a peaceful little sleep through the process." He reached over and stroked the baby's head—a prefab compassion that put me on edge.

"Next, we'll place some tiny, little patches on her chest. They are attached to an ECG monitor which will allow us to watch her little heartbeat." He turned his head, coughed slightly, and motioned to her legs. "Then I'll make the tiniest incision in the groin area. And with the help of a very special X-ray machine, I'll gently guide a little tube up into that wonderful little heart of hers."

There it was. Despite his transformation into Mr. Rogers, this man, who we barely knew, was about to jam something foreign through our baby's body and into her heart. But he wasn't through.

"From there I'll inject some dye so we can see how her blood is flowing and find out how we can help your little gift from heaven."

I glanced at my hands. My fingers were digging into my palms.

"How—" Amber swallowed. "How long?"

"The procedure itself?" He cleared his throat. "Less than thirty minutes."

She nodded and looked down to Billie-Jean asleep in her arms. Darlene sensed her need and rested a hand on her arm—while I, once again, missed my cue and sat like a lump.

"Alright then." The doctor rose and turned to Amber. "Would you like to accompany her back to the room with me?"

She nodded and he reached down to help her to her feet. We rose to follow but at the door, he turned to us. "She'll only be a moment."

I wasn't sure how to respond and asked, "Amber?"

She looked up from Billie-Jean and saw the expression on my face. "I'm okay," she said. Then, without another word, she turned and entered through the doorway.

The doctor gave me what was supposed to be a reassuring smile, "She'll be right back," and followed her inside—allowing the door to quietly shut behind him.

I stood in a long moment of silence before I heard Darlene sigh, "I need a smoke."

"A smoke?" I said. "When did you start?"

"In about thirty seconds."

CHAPTER
TWENTY

AMBER WAS BACK before Darlene had time to develop a habit. When she returned, her eyes were red but there were no tears. What a trooper. One day I look forward to taking lessons from her. She sat on the chair between Darlene and me. This time, for whatever reason, Darlene knew it best to give Amber her space. While I, on the other hand, thought it the perfect moment to be the sensitive uncle and take her hand—making us feel so awkward we were both grateful when she slipped it out of mine and back to her lap—proving once again my amazing gift at understanding women.

But sitting there doing nothing was more than I could bear, especially when I could be using the time to arm-wrestle God. Seriously, there was no better moment for a miracle. Picture it, Billie-Jean hooked up to a heart monitor and just before they begin, it suddenly shows there is nothing wrong. The perfect set-up. Even Dr. Martin would have to admit it was a bona fide miracle.

"Listen," I said to the women, "I think I'll step outside to clear my head."

Amber looked up. "Going on another one of your walks?" If there was any sarcasm it was softened by the gratitude in her eyes.

"Yeah." I rose and caught the two sharing a knowing smile. Apparently my Battle of Jericho tactics had been outed on their drive down. "It's a small building. I shouldn't be long."

Outside, it was warm and muggy—a bit unusual for this time of year. The news said a huge storm was on its way, complete with thunder and lightning—again, a bit unusual but nothing of concern. The building was tightly wedged between two others so I had to incorporate the entire block to circle it. No problem—though, after the first lap, I realized I might have been a bit overdressed in a sports coat and tie. Sadder still, I realized I had nothing new to pray. It was Yeshua, himself, who said, don't keep repeating the same thing over and over again since God already knows what we want.

So what was left?

I remembered a Buddhist friend in college who believed every time he spun a prayer wheel it released a prayer. As an engineering student he rigged a wheel up to solar power so it spun without his help. I'm not sure it made any difference or if his prayers were better answered on sunny days, but in some ways it felt like I was doing the same thing now.

By the second lap I even resorted to something the Bible calls, *tongues*. From what I'd read, it was best described as giving your brain a rest from having to search for the right words and simply relying on his Holy Spirit inside to utter a "spiritual language" that I didn't need to understand. Seems the apostle Paul in the New Testament was a big fan of it. And if it was good enough for him . . .

Did I feel foolish rattling off what sounded like gibberish? Absolutely. Was I careful to drop into stealth mode when passing others on the street? You bet. Did it do any good? Maybe. I felt a little better. I'm not sure. All I know is by round three, I'd even run out of my new "utterances" and was repeating them over and over again—which was okay, but how was that any different than repeating the same prayer in English over and over again?

For all intents and purposes, I'd run out of options. And though a miracle would be nice, I wasn't in the mood for another one of his audio-visual tours. Maybe it was my irritability from low blood sugar. If fasting was supposed to draw us closer, forget it. All I felt was the piling up of resentment. I was done with lectures. It was time for the delivery of goods.

But he's a clever God. On my third lap I noticed the church across the street and down the block. And the message board in front of it reading:

SACRIFICE OF PRAISE

"Enter his gates with thanksgiving and his courts with praise. Psalm 100:4"

Subtle, he was not. But did he actually expect me to start thanking him? Now? Now, when nothing had gone right? A "Sacrifice of Praise"? Really? Sorry, no sale. Not because I was stubborn. No. I simply refused to become a hypocrite. And if there was one thing I knew about Yeshua, he hated hypocrisy.

I'd just turned the corner when my phone rang. I saw Darlene's number and answered. "What's up?"

"You need to be here," she said.

"What's going on?"

"Now, Will." There was no missing the urgency in her voice. "We need you here now."

❧

By the time I returned, Dr. Martin was already seated with Amber and Darlene in the waiting room. When they looked up, I knew the news was bad.

"What's wrong?" I said. "How's the baby; is she okay?"

Martin rose to his feet and motioned to the empty chair. "Please, sit."

"What happened? What went wrong?"

"Nothing went wrong. The procedure went perfectly as planned."

"Then—"

"I'm afraid Billie-Jean's condition is worse than we expected."

The room shifted and I adjusted to keep my balance.

He motioned back to the chair. "Please."

I shook my head.

He continued. "The catheterization went as planned but once we reached her heart—"

I interrupted. "Tetralogy of Fallot; you said it was Tetralogy of Fallot."

"Yes. But of a severity, well to be quite frank, I've never seen it to this extent."

A faint sob escaped from Amber, barely discernable, but enough for Darlene to wrap an arm around her.

Martin began a detailed explanation, but I was straining too hard to read his tone and expressions to fully grasp what he said—until I heard: "You hadn't noticed her becoming more lethargic? Irritable? Breathing more rapidly than normal?"

My anger flared. "She's our first baby, how are we supposed to know what's normal?"

Another sob from Amber, and Darlene pulled her into her arms.

I continued, "*You're* the one who made us wait, then turned around and postponed things even longer."

"Yes," he cleared his throat, "we had an emergency."

"And this isn't?"

"It's not necessarily—"

"So what are you going to do? Can you fix it?"

He paused, waiting for me to take it down a notch. But I stood, glowering.

"Yes," he said. "To answer your question, it's most definitely treatable. But I suggest we operate as soon as possible."

"Operate?" The word slammed into my chest. Yes, I knew it was a possibility. But three weeks. Three weeks we'd been praying for a miracle and this is what we get? "When?" I demanded. "What does that mean?"

"I'll clear my schedule and—"

"What does that mean?"

"We'll see how she responds to this afternoon's sedative and if there are no ill effect—"

"*What does that*—"

He cleared his throat. "Tomorrow morning. I'd like to schedule her first thing in the morning."

He went on to rattle off the procedure, retreating to it like a wall of defense. But I barely heard. The room shifted again. Then again. Lack of food? Who knows. Whatever the reason, the empty chair now looked more inviting.

But I refused. Somebody had to take charge. And since it wasn't going to be God . . .

I turned to the doctor. "When will you know?"

"Know?"

"About the sedative. When will you know if she's strong enough to—"

"Two hours, maybe three. I suggest you grab a bite to eat and—"

"I'm staying here," Amber said, her voice muffled inside Darlene's embrace.

"It may be longer depending upon—"

"I'm staying here."

He turned to me and I nodded. "She stays." Then I added, "Can she go back there and sit with her?"

He hesitated.

"It's a simple question, Doctor. Can she sit with her baby while she recovers?"

"Yes."

Amber pulled from Darlene and wiped her face.

"There's one more thing," he said.

I looked at him—my patience gone.

"If she's ready," he cleared his throat. "If she's ready, I'd like to admit Billie-Jean to the hospital tonight."

"What?"

"To keep an eye on her. This will give us plenty of time to properly prep her before surgery."

"The hospital?" I said. "Tonight?"

"A precaution. To continue surveillance and to prepare her."

I felt all eyes turn to me, waiting for a decision. I hesitated, weighed the consequences, then gave my answer. "Yes."

CHAPTER
TWENTY-ONE

WITH AN EMPTY stomach going on thirty-two hours and twenty minutes—but who's counting—I already felt the first glass of wine. It didn't stop me from pouring the third.

"Whoa, easy there, cowboy," Darlene said from across the table.

"What?"

"Might want to ease up a bit."

I kept pouring. "Making up for lost time," I said. I doubt she knew what I meant, but I did. After six months of trying to get my act together I was through. And, no, this wasn't about breaking rules. It was about breaking friendship. Friendship? What a joke. Friends don't lead you on with promises they don't keep. They don't lead you down dark alleys and desert you.

The best to be said was Billie-Jean showed no adverse reaction to the sedative they used for the catheterization. So, with plenty of trepidation and Amber tears, we admitted her into the hospital. The good news was they had provisions for Amber to spend the night with Billie-Jean. The bad news was neither Darlene nor I were allowed to accompany her. I found a hotel up the street (expensive, we deserved it) and checked us into a couple rooms: at my insistence a suite for Darlene—a cheaper room for me.

Seeing how wrecked I was over Amber and the baby (she had no idea about Yeshua), Darlene suggested we forgo the hotel's restaurant and order in. A good idea. So, after showering, I headed down the hall to join her. I read it's smart to break a fast by eating something light, so I ordered a shrimp salad. I ignored the counsel about drinking.

Outside Darlene's 14th floor window, the night lights of Seattle sparkled like jewels. Sleek steel and glass high-rises surrounded us, their reflections shimmering off Lake Union. Not far away headlights and taillights snaked along I-5. And, disappearing into the approaching weather, was the white, luminous glow of the Space Needle.

We kept the room dimly lit—not for romance, but for the view.

"She'll be okay," Darlene repeated. "Dr. Martin has been doing these operations for years. He can be trusted."

"I'm glad there's somebody we can trust."

She cocked her head. "I'm guessing this is more than Billie-Jean?"

"What's the point?"

"Excuse me?"

"Of prayer? Of God?" She waited for me to continue and I didn't disappoint. "You said it yourself, just clap your hands and believe. What if he really is just a kid's fantasy? What if he's no more than some made-up boogieman to enforce our manmade philosophies?"

She looked at me a moment then measured her words. "For some people he's a lot more than that."

"And for some people the world's still flat."

"You are going through a tough patch."

"You think?"

"And a little drunk."

"Maybe . . . or maybe I'm finally sobering up. Seeing things as they really are." I set down the glass, nearly spilling it on the white, linen tablecloth then leaned back and pressed the heels of my palms against my eyes. "What did you do?"

"When . . ."

"When you lost your religion?" She gave no answer and I looked at her. "How did you cope?" I asked. "How did you feel?"

She eyed me another moment before answering. "Angry—betrayed."

I nodded, snorting in agreement.

"And," she added more softly, "I thought my heart would break." I frowned and she continued. "When I was a little girl, God was my knight in shining armor. My best friend forever. We shared *every* secret. And he was always there for me." She stared into her glass. Maybe it was the wine, maybe more, but for whatever reason I'd never seen her quite so vulnerable.

I nodded, then quietly said the obvious. "Until your uncle—the deacon."

"I cried, I begged, I pleaded."

"Did you ever . . ." I treaded softly here. "Did you ever think it was just a test? God's silence, I mean? That if you waited a bit longer, he'd have come to your rescue?"

She raised her eyes to mine, in both sorrow and contempt. I glanced away, sorry for my stupidity.

She finished her drink and she reached for the bottle that was nearly empty. "What was it Karl Marx said? Religion is the opium of the people?"

"But you quit," I said. "Cold turkey. No regrets."

She shook her head. "There's always regret. And, I suppose a little hope—the dream he'll somehow return, the emptiness refilled." A moment passed before she looked back to me. "And yes, I quit. Even for gullible little girls there's only so many times they can be betrayed."

I slowly nodded, thinking of our similarities. How many times could he have stepped in? Shown a little mercy? At least given me a clue? But, no. It was always, "trust me . . . have faith . . . just a little longer," as one opportunity after another slipped away. Not only for Billie-Jean, but for Amber—and Darlene. He talked about, *Your kingdom come.* Imagine what would have happened to her belief if she'd seen his power at work in all this? A loving God stepping in to save another helpless little girl?

Your kingdom come? No. Just another unanswered prayer.

So there we sat amidst the lies and broken promises. He spoke of broken bread? What about his broken word? The broken trust of a friend?

After a long moment, she said, "It's going to be a long night for you, isn't it?"

I nodded. "For you too."

She quietly mused. Then, focusing back on her glass she said, "My offer still stands, you know. Neither of us have to spend it alone."

I looked to her and she shrugged. We'd been down this road before. And though I always declined, more and more frequently I caught myself imagining what it would be like. But I always had something greater. Some*one* greater. Or so I thought. She tilted her head at me—not coquettishly, but a simple, honest inquiry from an honest heart. And no, she wasn't taking advantage of the situation. No more than I. This was something we'd both imagined, both needed— the touch and compassion of another.

Still, I was out of practice, unsure what to say. I didn't have to. As was often the case, Darlene sensed my thoughts. She set her glass on the table, touched the linen napkin to her mouth, and rose. "I'm going to freshen up a bit."

I nodded. As she passed, she touched my shoulder with an understanding hand. I stared ahead, watching her reflection in the window mixed with the lights of the city. Was there guilt? Of course. But I pushed it away. I wasn't the one who broke the relationship, who abandoned his friendship.

Lead us not into temptation?

I shook my head. You could cross that off the list too. I leaned back in the chair and closed my eyes against the growing tightness in my throat. Off in the distance, there was the soft rumble of approaching thunder.

CHAPTER

TWENTY-TWO

DARLENE HAD BARELY left the room before my phone rang. I pulled it from my pocket, saw Patricia's ID, and nearly hit *Cancel*. Then again, after all her time in prayer she deserved an update. "Hi," I said, making no attempt to sound cheery.

"What's the news?" she asked. "I've been waiting for your call. Is she going to be—"

Call it exhaustion, anger, or just plain spite, I pulled no punches. "They're operating tomorrow."

"*What?*"

"First thing in the morning." The blow left her speechless but I saw no need to soften it or serve as God's PR person. "It's worse than they suspected."

She paused a moment. "I don't understand. We prayed, we fasted."

"Yeah. We jumped through all the hoops." Another punch.

Another pause.

"Where are you now?"

"Still in Seattle, just down the street from the hospital."

"I'll be there in ninety minutes."

"Patricia, there's no need—"

"What hotel?"

"I really don't—"

"What hotel?"

"The Broadmoor, but—"

"Ninety minutes."

"Patricia, there's—"

She hung up. I pulled the phone from my face and held it a long moment before disconnecting. Everything was falling apart. Not the procedure or the doctors, they knew what they were doing. It was the loss of everything else.

Still holding the phone, I pressed my fingers against the burning of my eyes.

"Patty?" Darlene's voice asked.

I looked up and turned. She stood in the doorway, silhouetted by the glow from the bedroom light. I swiped at my eyes, clearing the emotion from my throat. "Yeah."

Another moment passed. Finally, she spoke. "I think we should call it a night."

"What?"

"There's no way I can compete."

"What? No, I told you, we're just friends."

She shook her head.

"What?"

"I'm not talking about her."

I scowled, losing her meaning. "Then . . .?"

"Seriously, are you that out of touch with your feelings?"

"What do you mean?"

"I'll see you in the morning, Will." She turned back to the bedroom.

"Darlene?"

"Goodnight."

"Dar—"

She entered and shut the door. I heard the soft click of a lock.

ᏬᎧ

I entered my own room and turned on the light just as my phone rang again. The ID read: "M. Carothers." The eccentric old neighbor with the treehouse.

I answered, "Mr. Carothers."

"What's wrong with you, can't you hear your dog?"

"Sorry. I'm down here in Seattle with my niece."

"No, you're not."

"Excuse me?"

"I can see that big screen TV of yours flickering from here."

Over the past years his conversations had become more and more disjointed so I let it go. "You said something about Siggy?"

"Fool thing's climbed the stairs to my treehouse and won't come down."

"Your—"

"Listen." I heard the phone rustle, a door or window slide open, followed by the sound of splashing water. In the distance there was barking. Siggy's. Non-stop and alarmed. "Hear him?"

"How'd he get out?"

"You tell me."

"Is that rain?"

"By the bucket. Wind and lightning too. No wonder he's scared."

"Can you—do you think you can coax him down?"

"Did I not mention the rain?"

"Right, but—"

"It's gonna get worse. Storm of the century, they say."

"If you could just—"

"I'm getting real tired of all the yapping. Keep it up and I'm calling the sheriff. Or them animal cruelty people. They got laws for this kind of thing, you know."

I rubbed my forehead, wandered to the window looking out over Lake Union. So far there was no rain, at least this far south. A pretty good chop to the water from the wind, but no rain. Not yet. Through the phone I continued hearing Siggy's barking—until it was drowned out by a loud clap and rolling boom.

Carothers chuckled, "That was a good one."

"You tried coaxing him down?"

"I told you, it's raining. Why he run up there in the first place is beyond me."

Of course, I knew. I also knew he wouldn't climb down. Not on his own.

"What about the Olsen kid?" I asked, referring to our neighbors. "Are they home?"

"It ain't my—" crackling static filled the phone. "Dang . . . that was—" and then the line went dead.

"Mr. Carothers? Mr. Carothers!"

I disconnected and called back. It rang once before a recording kicked in: "We're sorry, but all circuits are busy. Please hang up and try—"

I hung up and tried again.

One ring. Same recording.

I began to pace. I opened the directory on my phone, found the Olsens' number, and called.

"We're sorry, but all circuit are busy. Please—"

I hit redial, muttering, "Now what game are you playing? You're going to make me drive all the way up there and then back?"

"We're sorry, but all circuits are—"

I hung up and shoved the phone into my pocket. Grabbing my coat, I headed for the door.

જી

"Moron!"

I grimaced and shouted back through the closed car window, "Sorry!"

The pedestrian, an old woman with the overbite of a beaver, expressed her understanding by flipping me off. Not that I blamed her. I'd raced out of the parking garage onto the street, missing her by mere inches—and scaring the daylights out of both of us. Was it the booze? In part. But I suspected more.

Somehow I got onto the freeway and headed north, weaving my way through insensitive drivers who insisted on traveling the speed limit. The chance of making the last ferry out of Anacortes at eleven o'clock was up for grabs. And getting on board this time of year without a reservation made the odds next to impossible. So, I reached for my phone, got their number, and gave a call.

After working my way through the myriad of, "Press this number for that, and that number for this," I finally got a real person and explained my emergency. "It's my octogenarian grandfather. He's lost outside in the storm! He called, begged for help just before the island lost phone service." (Alright, the grandfather bit was a lie, but Siggy is eleven, which is almost eighty in dog years.) Regardless, it worked. She said, if possible, they'd hold a place for me.

Fat drops of rain splatted onto my windshield near Lynwood. By the time I passed the Arlington exit, it was coming down hard. And, yes, Yeshua and I had a few choice words. Actually, I had the words. If he had something to say, I was in no mood to listen—though you can't fault him for trying. Somewhere between Burlington and Anacortes I started hearing voices that sounded like a shouting mob.

I glanced to the radio, but of course it was off.

"He saved others!" the voices cried. "Let him—"

"No!" I yelled over the crowd, the beating wipers, and the pounding rain. Once or twice in the past I'd tried cutting him off, but this time I was serious. Call it vengeance, call it self-preservation. Whatever the case, I would not cave in and let him have his way. "No!"

"Come down off that—"

"NO!" I shouted. "This is my free will! Respect it! I don't want this! Do you hear me? I don't want *you*!"

And for the first time, after all these days, my prayer was answered. The sounds of the mob began to fade. By the time I reached the ferry terminal—where a wiry attendant who could barely stand against the wind escorted me to the front of the line—the voices ended.

All of them.

TWENTY-THREE

ONCE I WAS on the island, my wipers could no longer keep up with the rain. Gusts of wind swamped the windshield with sheets of water so thick it was impossible to see—even when lightning filled the sky. Hunched over the wheel, peering out, I dropped my speed to a crawl, just to see the road, not to mention navigating the flooded areas and fallen trees. I counted three of them down. One cedar barely left enough room to squeeze past, its branches scraping along the passenger side. What had Carothers said, the storm of the century? I don't know about that, but it was one of the worst I'd seen.

We still had power—at least at the ferry terminal. But by the time I reached the center of the island, all houses along the road were dark. Fifteen minutes later, as I approached my mailbox, I saw the same was true with my place—except for the glare of headlights from a pickup parked in the driveway.

What on earth? I slowed to a stop, wiper blades flying, rain thrumming the roof. I eased down the driveway toward the house. In a flash of lightning, I noticed an unlit vehicle beside the pickup. Chip's Jeep. I parked in front of it and opened my door, stepping out into the storm. I turned my head away from the stinging rain and sloshed toward the back kitchen door just as Dylan, Chip's theater partner, emerged. He wore a heavy peacoat, Seahawks stocking cap, and a backpack slung across one shoulder.

Spotting me, he came to a stop and yelled over the rain. "Will!" Then to me, "What are you doing here?"

"What are you?"

"Aren't you supposed to be in Seattle—your niece or something?"

I could tell he'd been drinking, but that was all I could tell. "What are you doing in my house?" I shouted.

He laughed and adjusted his backpack. "Chip's inside. He can explain."

I motioned to the backpack. "What's in there?"

"This? Just stuff." He grinned as lightning flickered across his wet face.

"Whose?" I shouted.

More laughter. "Funny." He headed to the truck when thunder pounded the air, loud and long. "Chip's inside," he called. "He can explain everything."

I hesitated then turned for the kitchen.

"Still got a couple cold ones in the fridge," he yelled. "If you're interested."

Stomping off the rain, I entered the kitchen. On the counter sat two pizza boxes, extra-large, open and empty.

I called, "Chip?"

No answer.

I moved into the dark living room and turned for the hallway when I saw the darting beam of a flashlight. It came from the nursery. "Chip?"

I started down the hall just as he appeared. "Will?"

"What's going on?"

"Yeah. Me and Dylan, we were just doing a little house sitting for you." He adjusted a backpack of his own. "Amber said you'd be gone for the night and with the storm and everything we figured it wouldn't hurt to swing by and check up on the place."

"And have a few beers and pizza."

He flipped his hair to the side and grinned. "You've got Netflix."

I wasn't amused. "How'd you get in?"

"Amber, she made a key. You know, for emergencies. Like this. So, what's the news on Billie-Jean. Phones are out, so I haven't—"

"I think you should go."

"Oh, right. Sure, no problem." He started down the hall and I stepped aside to let him pass. "We were just heading out, anyway."

"What were you doing in the nursery?"

"Just, you know . . ."

I didn't and moved to see.

"We'll pick up everything," he called back. "Good as new. You won't even know we were here."

Inside the nursery, the emergency night light I'd installed had done its job; kicking on at the loss of power. It cast light and shadows across the dozens of unused baby gifts we'd shoved in there. Nothing had been touched; everything was in its usual disarray—except the opened and shattered glass door of my bookcase.

"Chip!" I moved to investigate. The shelves were empty. Stripped bare. I spun back to the door and raced into the hall. "Chip!" He was gone. I ran down the hallway and into the kitchen where he'd left the door standing open.

Outside in the rain, he was chasing Dylan's truck up the driveway, its wheels spinning and sliding in the mud and gravel. "Dylan!" he yelled. But the truck didn't slow as it finally bounced up onto the road, fishtailing to the right and disappearing into the storm. "Dylan!"

I ran into the wind and rain shouting, "What are you doing? Are those my books?"

He looked left then right for an escape. The Jeep would do him no good, I'd blocked it with my car. He could try the road, but how far could he get before I caught up to him in my car? Trapped, with no alternative, he raced back down the driveway at me. I braced myself, but he veered to the right and darted for the side of the garage. He was rounding the house, heading for the beach.

I took off after him. "Chip!"

The side of the garage was dark and muddy. The slick, wooden steps leading to the beach were no better. I was halfway down when my foot shot out from under me. I barely caught myself, grabbing the old, wood railing, but paid the price by once again throwing out my back—and jamming a large, ugly sliver deep into the palm of my hand. By the time I reached the bottom and staggered onto the beach, Chip was lost in the wind, ocean spray, and rain—until lightning strobed across the sky and I spotted him thirty yards ahead, still running.

"Chip!" He couldn't hear me. I barely heard myself. I started after him, wind and rain biting my face—every step sending a shock through my back. But that was my house he had violated. My books he was stealing—worth tens of thousands of dollars! *Forgive our debtors?* Ha! I tried and look where it got me—lies, broken promises, betrayal. And not only from Chip.

More lightning flashed and I saw Chip looking over his shoulder. He spotted me and continued running. So did I. But it wasn't long before I was out of breath, my lungs burning for air.

And still I pressed on, shouting, "Chip!" (And a few other phrases I'm not proud to be repeating.)

I suppose, if there was any grace, if God showed the slightest whim of caring, it was when I heard Siggy. I was parallel to old man Carothers's place—his treehouse off to my right in the woods. Either because Siggy never stopped barking or because he heard my voice and started up again, his pleas for help cut through the storm and reached my ears. Gasping, fighting for breath, I thought of ignoring him and continuing the chase. The books cost a fortune. Then again, so did a heart attack.

I'd eventually find the kid, I knew that. It was a small island and I knew where he lived. And Siggy needed my help now. Still seething, I slowed and turned. I angled my way up the beach and hobbled over the small berm. The barking continued as I waded through the wet undergrowth of ferns and salal until, in another burst of lightning, I spotted him. He stood at the top of the treehouse stairs, soaked and shivering.

"Hey fella!" I shouted. "What're you doin' here?"

He wagged his tail but continued shaking. It was more than just the rain and cold. The poor thing was terrified. And exhausted—physically and mentally. I knew the feeling.

I arrived at the foot of the steps and called, "It's okay, fella. I'm here, you'll be okay."

He whined.

"Come on down. I'm here. You've done this before. C'mon."

He whimpered, he whined, he paced but he would not obey.

I grew sterner. "C'mon! Siggy, come on down!"

Nothing.

"Now! I'm not kidding!"

Neither was he.

Finally, with an oath, I took the first step. My back screamed with such pain, I dropped to my hands and knees, reduced to climbing each stair like a four-legged animal. But at least I was here, doing what I could—showing more compassion for my dog than what was shown toward me.

At least *I* was faithful.

TWENTY-FOUR

I'D READ OF something like this before; they call it a micro-burst—a mini-tornado, a storm within a storm. Or in my case: adding insult to injury. I'd just carried Siggy down one torturous step after another and was leaning over, fighting the pain, when it hit—straight off the ocean, wind so fierce it was impossible to stand. I dropped to the ground, pulling Siggy in close, turning him from the storm, burying my face into his fur. Over the roar I heard branches cracking, flying past us. Realizing the danger, I rose and, against the wind and debris, pulled Siggy with me under the steps for cover.

Barely hearing my own voice, I shouted into the gale, "What are you doing!?"

Of course, there was no answer.

We stayed hunkered down like that two, maybe three, minutes before the burst stopped as suddenly as it started. Now we simply faced your normal, everyday storm of the century.

And heard a voice.

Not mine and not Yeshua's. It came from that small marsh separating Carothers's place from mine. So faint, I thought it a trick of the wind until I noticed Siggy had perked up his ears in that direction.

"What is it, boy?"

More curious than wise, I rose to my feet and carefully hobbled toward the sound. Branches, large and small, lay everywhere, flattening the ferns and undergrowth. Siggy was spooked and stayed glued to my side. I counted four, five fallen trees—some pushed over in the loose, soggy soil, others snapped in two.

As we approached the marsh, the voice grew louder, clearer—until I could make out words: "Help me . . . somebody . . .!"

We reached the soggy bank and, in the next flash of lightning, saw Chip. He lay in the water on his back, pinned by a fallen tree, his neck stretched up to keep his head out of the salty brine. "Help me!" He spit rain from his mouth. "I can't get it off!"

"Slide under!" I shouted. "Hold your breath and—"

"I can't get it off!"

"Try to squirm and—"

"Help me!"

Seeing no alternative and again swearing under my breath, I stepped into the icy, cold water and waded toward him. Fortunately, the tide was out, bringing the water no higher than my knees. I glanced back to Siggy who had the good sense to remain on shore. The tree pinning Chip was a thick Douglas Fir, a good eighteen inches in diameter. It lay diagonally across his chest.

"I'm stuck!" He twisted and kicked, but only managed to create waves washing around his neck and lower jaw.

I arrived, searching for a solution.

"The tide's rising!" he shouted.

"Don't worry! We'll get you out!" I planted my feet in the muck and stooped down. I wrapped my arms around the tree and nearly passed out in pain as I tried to lift it— then pull it—then push it. But it wouldn't budge. Thinking I could dig him out, I dropped to my knees, bringing the water up to my waist. I reached under and groped, slipping my hand between his back and the muddy bottom. But there was only three inches of sludge before I hit hard, packed dirt.

I struggled and rose. I turned toward the woods. Carothers's house lay fifty yards to my left, Olsen's another hundred after that.

Reading my thoughts, he cried out with a bit of melo-drama, "Don't leave me here! I don't want to die alone!"

"Nobody's going to die!" I shouted. But as I looked at the size of the tree, the water so close to his mouth, and the rising tide, a knot formed in my gut. He might be right.

He saw my expression and cried again, "Please! Please don't leave me!"

I scanned the marsh, the shore. There had to be a solution. He was starting to shake. It could be the cold, it could be shock—or the muscles in his outstretched neck were growing so fatigued they were giving out. I cupped my hand, the bad one with the splinter, under his head for him to rest on it.

"I'm sorry, man," he whimpered. "We did it for the theater." He spit more rain from his mouth. "I planned to pay you back, just as soon as we—"

"Quiet. We'll talk later." But, even as I spoke, as I watched the water slowly creeping up, I wondered if that would even be possible.

"C'mon," I angrily muttered. "Give us a break—C'mon!"

Chip frowned. "Are you praying?"

"I . . . yeah."

"Pray for me too."

I scoffed. He looked at me and I explained. "I'm no good at that. Not now."

"The Our Father." He coughed. "You know the Our Father, right?"

I looked at him startled. "What?"

"I'm Catholic. My mom made me say it."

"I—don't . . ."

"You know it?"

"Yeah, but—"

"Say it. Please . . ." He moved his head, trying to stretch more out of the water. "Please . . ."

He saw my hesitation. Then began on his own, "Our Father . . ."

I looked down, staring at the water that had risen to the base of his chin. What had Yeshua said about God loving his children as a Father? Did that include lapsed Catholics? I had no idea.

"Please, Will . . ."

I took a breath and finally repeated, "Our Father."

He continued, "Whose ark's in . . ." He scowled. "How's it go?"

"Who *art* in heaven," I said—my mind racing to Yeshua's words about God's kingdom being wherever God is king. But . . . *Even here? Even now?*

"Who art in heaven," Chip repeated my words and looked to me waiting for more.

I continued. "Hallowed be your name."

As he repeated the phrase, my jaw tightened. How was it possible? How could God's name possibly be hallowed— how could he be praised in something like this?

Chip anxiously looked to me. I forced out the next sentence: "Your kingdom come, your will be done on earth as it is in heaven."

The water had reached the top of his chin, lapping around the corners of his mouth. Through pursed lips he repeated my words.

How? I thought. *How can your kingdom come like this? How can your will be done?*

He finished and waited for more.

I obliged. "Give us this day our daily bread."

Lightning flickered. Even in the rain, I saw tears slipping from his eyes, felt my own burning. He repeated my words, mouth closed against the water, lips barely moving.

I pushed on. "And forgive us our debts as we—" The phrase stuck in my throat; the irony suddenly apparent— "as we forgive our debtors."

A tiny ripple washed over his mouth, splashed into his nose. And another, bigger. He began to cough. I pulled on his neck with everything I had, my back searing in white-hot pain, as I gave him those precious few millimeters to cough, to gag . . . and to take his final breath.

He looked up at me and I practically spat out the words. "Lead us not into temptation, but deliver us from evil."

His mouth and nose submerged. I pulled harder but it was no use. I knew it, and so did he. But instead of panicking, he seemed to relax, giving in to his fate. He closed his eyes, then leaned back into my hand, letting the water wash over his face.

"No!" I shouted. I braced myself, pulled harder on his neck. "You will not give up! Chip! NO!"

"What in Sam hill?"

I turned to see the outline of an old man standing on the bank. "Carothers!" I shouted.

"Your mutt here stopped barking. Figured with all that wind he got himself hurt or killed. What are you doing?"

"He's trapped," I shouted.

"I can see that."

"Give me a hand. Help me move this tree."

"I ain't going in there."

"He's drowning!"

"No way you and me can move that thing." He turned to leave, lightning flickering across his back.

"You can't go!"

"I'm fetching the Olsens!" he shouted.

"There's no time! Carothers? Carothers!"

He disappeared into the night. And, as thunder clapped, exploding around us, the sound of the mob from my car returned. Relentless.

TWENTY-FIVE

"HE TRUSTS IN God, let God deliver him!"

I looked down at Chip, seeing if he heard. But of course, he hadn't. He remained in my hand, relaxed, mouth shut, eyes closed.

"No!" I violently shook him and his eyes popped open. "You will not die!"

I heard another voice over the shouting mob: *"My God, my God, why have you forsaken me?"*

Lightning strobed, silhouetting trees, and suddenly I'm there, at the foot of the cross. There are a dozen others, taunting, hurling insults. I'm there, and I'm not. I'm standing in the marsh looking up at his face beaten beyond recognition—nose broken, eye swollen shut, everything soaked in blood. I'd been here before, months ago. But the horror is magnified a thousand times because suddenly . . .

I'm also with him, up on the cross. I'm stripped naked, my skin shredded, my flesh flayed—every inch of my body shrieks in pain as I hang from my hands, his hands, feeling the searing burn of iron spikes driven through my shattered bones, his bones.

"Let's see if Elijah saves him!"

I can't breathe. I'm suffocating. As if I'm under water with Chip. But no, it's the weight of my hanging body, it's squeezing the air out of my lungs, making it impossible to catch my breath.

"If you're the son of God come down from there!"

"He saved others, let him save himself!"

I'm back in the marsh, looking up. I'm on the cross, pushing the weight of my body down upon broken, spike-impaled feet, rising just enough to suck in a breath. Back in the marsh I'm looking down at Chip, his mouth submerged, eyes open, now terrified, panicked at his own death. And I know what I have to do. With my free hand I reach to his nose and pinch it shut. He writhes and thrashes, no doubt thinking it's a mercy kill.

"No!" I shout. "No!" I lower my head and shove my face into the cold water. My mouth searches and finds his. I press my lips against his lips. The breath, the very breath I had fought to breathe up on the cross, Yeshua fought to breathe, I blow out.

Chip is shocked. Refuses. But only for a moment until realization sets in. He opens his mouth allowing me to blow my breath into him. My breath, our breath, becoming his breath.

"*You who were going to destroy the temple and build it in three days!*"

I yank my face out of the water and I'm back on the cross fighting through impossible pain as I push down on my destroyed feet.

"*Come down from that cross and we'll believe you!*"

I swallow back a scream, as I, as *we,* struggle to rise, finally sucking in another breath.

I'm back in the marsh staring up at Yeshua through the pounding rain.

"*Father, forgive them, they don't know what they're doing!*"

Up on the cross, we suck in another breath, a fraction of what we had before since our feet can no longer sustain the pain, and we collapse. I look down, see Chip. Back in the marsh, with our precious air, I shove my face into the frigid water. This time he eagerly accepts my mouth as I blow breath into him. My breath. Yeshua's breath. I remember Yeshua and the balloon analogy he used the first time I met him. His life entering mine. Mine entering Chip's.

"*Father forgive him, he doesn't know what he's doing!*" The words have changed. Forgive *him?* Forgive Chip? His theft, his betrayal? As the boy's lungs fill with our air, I'm still thinking of the balloon. His Spirit entering, pushing back, replacing my death. Chip's death. With his life.

Your kingdom come.

I pull my face from the water, desperate for another breath, pushing against our broken feet to gulp in a fraction of air. Chip continues to panic. He needs the air more than me. More than Yeshua. I shove my face into the black water and find his mouth.

Forgive us our debts—

Suddenly, I'm back in the Arlington hospital having my meltdown, then Seattle, raging at Dr. Martin, then in my car fighting Yeshua. I pull from the water, lungs burning for breath—his breath, my breath, our breath.

How long this continues, I'm not certain—fighting for wisps of air and then giving them up. But with each and every breath we struggle to take and share I feel a change. Barely perceptible, but a change.

In time, I hear Siggy barking. I turn my head and see Carothers arriving with Joel Olsen, a tall Swede, and his thirteen-year-old kid.

"He dead?" Carothers shouts.

I shake my head then fill my lungs and dive back under the water. It's too dark and deep to see Chip but his mouth is always there, anxious, and desperate.

As we forgive our debtors.

When I resurface, the father and son have waded in and are trying in vain to move the tree. I gulp another breath and go under. Their work is not my concern. I find Chip's mouth and blow into it.

Your kingdom come—

Resurfacing, I hear a chain saw fire up. Olsen and his boy have positioned themselves around the tree and are cutting into it. The saw groans, jams, stops, and starts. I drop back under to share another breath.

Your will be done.

I return to the surface as father and son shout to one another, pushing against the tree with all their might—until it gives way and they shove it aside.

I yank Chip to the surface. He comes up gagging and spewing water. Before he's even finished, he turns and throws his arms around me—with such force we both tumble back into the marsh. He laughs and I swear as he pulls me to my feet for another embrace, more powerful than before, which, despite the pain . . . I do my best to endure.

TWENTY-SIX

THEY CARTED CHIP off to our island's medical center with what they guessed to be a broken rib or two. I headed back to the house to get some rest—i.e., take a hot shower, change clothes, and pace the floor waiting for the morning's first ferry back to the mainland. The phones were still out, not that mine had any chance of working thanks to all the water. I regretted giving up our land line, despite the fact there would be little news at 3:30 in the morning. And my books, my treasures? I suppose I'd eventually go back and search for them, though I suspect they were already becoming part of the marsh's ecosystem.

By the time I'd caught the ferry and crossed over, the thick clouds took on the dull glow of what we call sunrise. I had so much to process. So many things had happened in that marsh to Chip and me—God things—I was unsure how to begin. I figured prayer would be the best place, particularly with the upcoming operation, but I didn't want to drop into my habit of repetitive begging.

I recalled the church reader board suggesting we enter God's presence with praise, the same instruction Yeshua had given. *Hallowed be your name.* But I was too tired to make a list of things to appreciate—which, in my case, would be very short as I still had plenty to work out. I figured maybe a song wouldn't hurt. They do that in church. Unfortunately, the only hymn I knew was "Amazing Grace." And after the fifth or sixth time (I only knew the first verse), it got as repetitive as my begging.

Somewhere north of Mount Vernon I noticed I'd picked up a passenger. He sat in the seat beside me wearing his signature robe and sandals.

Self-conscious of my singing, I asked, "How long have you been there?"

"Me? I never left. Catchy song."

"I can't carry a tune in a bucket."

"I've noticed. Still, when it comes to praise, it's not the voice I listen to."

"Right," I said, unable to hide my cynicism.

"Sounds like there's an unbeliever in our midst."

I chose not to say what I was thinking—as if that ever did any good.

"You know, Will, praise is not kissing up to me." (See what I mean?) "It's not chanting incantations to make me show up."

"I didn't—"

"It's aligning yourself to what's real so *you* show up."

"Aligning," I said. "Patricia's minister used that same word."

"Imagine that."

I was too exhausted to debate theology, particularly with the Creator of the Universe, so I cut to the chase. "How's it help Billie-Jean?"

He gave no answer.

"Am I just supposed to keep rattling off thank-yous even when I don't feel like it? Isn't that lying and hypocrisy which you hate?"

"What's true, versus the truth. We've talked about this before, you know."

Enlighten me, I silently thought.

He did. "Praise is the real truth. Your feelings are the lie." I held my tongue and he continued, "Once you see truth, once you're connected to it, we can get down to business." I kept silent but he wouldn't let it go. "Have you read about Jehoshaphat yet?"

"Jehoshaphat?" I said. "Someone actually named their kid, Jehoshaphat?"

"Don't blame me. Free will, remember?"

I snorted.

"As the king of Israel, his army was surrounded not by one, not by two, but by three hostile forces, all bent on his destruction."

Welcome to my world, I thought.

"Good point," he said, then continued, "but instead of fighting them, he instructed his people to start worshipping."

"They were surrounded by three armies and he told them to worship?"

Yeshua nodded. "And they obeyed."

"And . . .?"

"Not a one of his people was hurt."

I shot him a skeptical look.

"You want to see?"

"No, no," I quickly replied. "I'm good right here."

He chuckled and continued. "Each of the three armies turned against one another and completely wiped themselves out. So much so it took the people three days to collect all the loot and spoils of war."

"So . . . you're saying praise is a weapon?"

"I'm saying, *'Hallowed be his name.'*"

I gave a grudging nod. It was a nice story, but I wasn't going to be sidetracked. "So, are you going to heal Billie-Jean or not?"

"*'Your kingdom come, your will be—'*"

"Will you stop that!" The outburst surprised both of us; well, at least me. Yeshua sat calmly in silence waiting for me to compose myself.

"Sorry," I said, "I'm a little tired."

"You should be exhausted."

I took a long breath. "Look, I know something happened back there, something huge with Chip—and probably me. But what about Billie-Jean? Are you going to be with her?"

"I am now."

I tried again, measuring my words. "Is she going to be okay?"

"Isn't that what you've been praying?"

"I've been praying about a lot of things."

"And you've been getting answers."

"If you count no an answer."

"My answers are always yes, Will. Yes and amen."

"As usual then, I'm sure it's all my fault, because I'm not seeing it."

"My ways are not your ways."

I threw him a look then quoted from our past conversation. "You've got all those 'moving parts.'"

He smiled. "More than you know."

We were getting nowhere. So, again, I chose to remain silent. But like I said, he's no good at letting things go.

"Talk to me, Will."

I shook my head.

"Come on."

I blew out a breath.

"Think of this as prayer."

Finally, I answered. "It's just—why do you always have to be so oblique, so . . . obscure?"

"Why are you so blind?"

I fought to keep my voice even. "I'm talking about Billie-Jean. Are you going to answer my prayers for her or not?"

"More than you can imagine."

"What does that mean? Why can't you just give me a straight answer, yes or no?"

"I'm not binary, remember?"

I took another breath and blew it out in frustration.

He answered, "You're always looking at a single thread as the answer."

"What should I be looking at?"

"The entire tapestry. That's what I weave. Beautiful, breathtaking tapestries. Each a work of art."

I turned to him.

"Sometimes the single threads are bright and cheery. Other times they're dark and confusing. But each and every one is necessary to complete my masterpiece."

"Masterpiece?"

"Yes. A masterpiece for all of creation to admire. The one I call . . . Will Thomas."

I was stunned, had no idea how to respond. But, of course, there was no need. Because when I turned to him, he was gone.

☙

Ninety minutes later, thanks to traffic, I pulled into the hospital's garage. Of course, I drove up the wrong ramp, the one leading to the doctor and employee's area. And, of course, I had to turn around, explain to the attendant I was an idiot, and re-enter the area designated for visitors. Not, of course, without paying the minimum charge of six dollars.

Wandering down the halls on foot and asking for help, I finally found the correct waiting room. Like Martin's office, it was designed to feel homey—table lamps, a large throw rug, two sofas, and a spattering of unmatched easy chairs. Darlene sat at one end of the room, eyes closed. Patricia sat at the other, her long legs curled under her in the chair. There was no sign of Amber. Spotting me, Patricia unfolded herself, and rose to join me. I saw she'd been crying.

"What's going on?" I said. "Where's Amber?"

"There's a problem." She reached for my arm then thought better of it.

"What kind of problem?"

"They took her away—for consultation."

I stiffened. "Consultation? Why didn't you go with her?"

"Not allowed," Darlene called from her chair. "We're not her guardians. You could have, but you didn't seem to be around."

"Why didn't you call?" Patricia asked.

"Long story." My heart began to pound. I felt the familiar tightening around my chest. *What are you doing now?* I thought. *I've got nothing left! What!?* I looked over to Darlene and asked, "Where did they take her?"

She shook her head and I turned to Patricia. She had no answer either. This time she did reach out to take my arm. "I think we should pray."

I yanked it away. "Pray? *Pray?*" Before she could answer, I turned and headed for the door.

"Where're you going?" Darlene called.

"To find my niece. To get some answers." I stormed out of the room and crossed the hall to the nurse's station. "Where's Dr. Martin? Where's my niece?"

The nurse, a stout woman with thin whisps of gray hair, looked up from her charts. "Your—"

"My niece. Amber, Ambrosia Driscoll?"

"They're in consultation."

"I know that! But where?" My heart was hammering in my ears.

"I'm sorry. We're not at liberty—"

"I'm her uncle, her guardian! Where are they?"

"Sir, if you don't lower your voice, I'll have to call security."

"If I don't lower my—" I stopped. Then turned. Searching the hall, I chose a direction, any direction, and started off.

"Sir . . ." she called after me. "Sir . . ."

Realizing I was giving an encore of my Arlington hospital performance, I slowed, then spotted a restroom to my left. I turned and entered.

The door had barely shut before I was shouting, "Why? What do you want now?" I began pacing, trapped like an animal, like Siggy up on those stairs—back and forth from wash counter to stall. "I give and I give and all you do is take! How many times have I asked you to heal her? How many times have I begged you to do something, *anything*?" I punched the stall door. It flew open and back at me. "Is this how you get your jollies, torturing children, teasing your little pets?" I was back at the sink, leaning over the counter. "Is it? *Is it!?*"

There was a knock on the door. "Will?" It was Patricia.

"Kinda busy here!"

"The doctor's back. He wants to talk to you."

I slammed both fists on the counter and crossed to the door. I threw it open, passed Patricia, refusing to let her dish out any more platitudes, and headed for the waiting room. When I arrived Amber was there, face streaked with tears. Seeing me, she raced from the doctor's side and into my arms. "Uncle Will . . ."

Taken aback, I held her, felt her body trembling.

"It's okay." I choked. "We'll get through this—whatever it is, we'll get through it." She clung tighter, burying her face into my chest. "It's okay," I whispered.

I looked over to Darlene—her own face wet with tears. And then to the doctor. "What is it now?" I demanded.

He shook his head.

"What?"

"It's the darndest thing," he said. "We were getting ready, prepping her, when," he cleared his throat, "when the technician noticed a change in her heart rhythm."

"What does that mean?"

"I had no idea, none of us did, so I ordered an echo gram."

"And?"

"We still have to run some tests—"

"What are you saying, doctor?"

He coughed. "It appears Billie-Jean's heart is perfectly normal."

"It's what!?" I turned to Darlene who was wiping her eyes and nodding—as Amber pulled her face from me and looked up, beaming through her tears.

"It's a miracle, Uncle Will. A miracle."

While behind me, ever so softly, I heard Patricia whispering, "Thank you, Jesus . . . thank you."

TWENTY-SEVEN

"HEY LITTLE ONE, it's been quite a ride, hasn't it?"

If Billie-Jean heard, she was too busy working her bottle to answer. Which was fine with me. Here, in the pre-dawn light of the alcove and with the muffled lap of waves below, I was content just gazing down at her, marveling at the delicate intricacies—those tiny fingernails, now perfect in color, and don't even get me started on her eyelashes. Seriously, if holding her like this was all there was to heaven, sign me up.

But all good things come to an end . . .

"I thought you had work?"

I looked up to see Amber—groggy, unkept in baggy sweats and Seahawk's T shirt. "Yeah," I softly said, "I do."

"Well here." She reached for the baby. "Don't want to be late."

I reluctantly handed over Billie-Jean. As the mother, Amber had first dibs, but I planned to be a close second.

Over the past days life gradually returned to normal. Billie-Jean was still going in for a checkup or two, but as far as they could tell, she was perfectly healthy. No one knew why. But of course, everyone did.

Darlene and Patricia returned to school. And, although keeping their distance, Amber and Darlene were allowing Patricia to become more and more a part of the family. Family? Not exactly my definition, then again I seemed to have little say in the matter. Even Chip was working his way back into our good graces. Slowly. But working his way. So much had happened since Billie-Jean's birth. Actually, since Christmas Eve when Amber stood at my front door, dripping wet—the same evening Yeshua began his special guest appearances. It felt as if I'd been dropped into some sort of fast-track graduate program, taking courses in a subject I knew nothing about.

Two hours later, I pulled onto the sprawling grounds of the Snohomish Correctional Institute. I parked the car and stared at the imposing structure—the towers, the high chain link fence, the razor wire. *What are you up to now?* I thought. I turned off the ignition, opened my door . . . and stepped into hot, Middle Eastern sun, so bright I had to shield my eyes.

"Come on, Will, keep up."

I turned to see Yeshua passing by, traipsing up a steep, rocky path. He wore the same white robe I saw in Galilee after his resurrection. Behind him followed a small group of people, many I recognized as his disciples. And down below, off to our right, rose a walled, first-century city.

He moved so quickly I had to scramble to catch up. Once I arrived, breathing heavily, I motioned over to the city. "Jerusalem?"

"That's right."

I looked back to the people behind us, the hill before us, then his dazzling-white robe. "The Ascension?" I asked. "Is this where you go to heaven?"

"You *have* been reading." We continued walking and I worked to keep up pace with him. "So how's the job?" he asked.

"My *daily bread*?"

He threw me a smile.

"No, I get it," I said. "And that's cool. You want me to go into that prison and convert everyone to Christianity, right?"

He chuckled, shaking his head.

"What?"

"I'm not a club, Will. I don't want people signing up for Club Christ."

"Of course you do; that's what you've said."

"No. I said preach the good news and make disciples. *Disciples*, Will. Big difference. And you'll definitely have your chance." The climb grew steeper and I breathed harder. "But that's only part of what's coming."

"Coming? Are you telling me there's something more?"

He grinned. "What's your greatest desire? What have you wanted to do ever since you were a kid?"

"Be a rock star?"

"I heard you sing, remember?"

He had a point.

"I'm serious," he said. "What gives you the greatest satisfaction?"

"I was doing it at the University."

"No, you weren't."

"I wasn't?"

"You were teaching what you love. Not doing it."

I turned to him, waiting for more. But like so many times, he remained silent, letting me work it out until, slowly, the light came on. "Wait . . . you're not thinking I should—you're not talking about writing?"

"Isn't that your passion?"

"Well, yeah, but—"

"Delight yourself in the Lord and I'll give you the desires of your heart."

"So, what—I'm like getting some kind of reward for being good?"

"No. You're finally coming into alignment."

I frowned, trying to understand.

"Ever stop to think maybe we gave you your passion in the first place?"

"You? But—"

"We just had to straighten it out a little so you can use it."

"But—I . . ."

"'—*can do all things through Christ who strengthens you.*' Another one of my favorite verses."

My mind raced. "You don't understand, I've tried. Over and over again but—it's just never worked out."

"Maybe you never found something worth writing about."

"Like . . .?"

"What were you thinking a moment ago—about being in a graduate course?"

"That's true, but—"

"Might be time for that doctorate thesis."

I blinked, scowled. "You want me to write about . . . *this*? About *us*?

"What do you always tell your students, 'Write what you know'?"

"Yes. But there's so *little* I do know. I don't want to be contrary—"

"Contrary? You?" There was that trademark grin. "Listen, I want you to hang back a bit. I need to say goodbye to these folks before I leave."

I nodded, still trying to process what I heard.

"And trust me, combined with this next season, you'll have plenty to write."

"Another season? Great."

He laughed. "It will be." He slapped me on the shoulder and turned to finish the climb, but not before calling back, "The greatest one yet!"

I slowed to a stop and watched as the crowd swarmed around me and followed him the last several paces to the top of the hill. Was he serious? To write down all that happened over the past months? I certainly had enough material. But what about finding time? Then again, with only a twenty-hour work week . . . I shook my head. He'd definitely been setting things up.

I paused to think over what we'd covered the last few weeks—just on prayer alone. Particularly, his prayer, the Lord's Prayer:

Our Father in heaven – Well, he certainly made that part clear.

Hallowed be your name – "Enter his courts with praise." Check. Whether I feel like it or not. Double check.

Your kingdom come – I mused a moment over Chip— still as obnoxious as ever and always quick to challenge what little I knew about God. But at least he was asking. Same with Amber. And Darlene? Something had happened to her in the hospital—Darlene Pratford, always the enigma, and one I could never quite get out of my mind. And what was going on with Patricia's growth? I shook my head. What did Yeshua say, "So many moving parts"?

Your will be done on earth as it is in heaven – Who on earth could have dreamed up these last few weeks. Then again, maybe it wasn't dreamed up on earth. "I'm giving you a tapestry," he said, "not a thread." I understood. But what about this business of being his masterpiece? He obviously didn't know who he was working with.

Give us this day our daily bread – Eating of him daily? I get it. And if he wanted broken bread—me making a living teaching in some prison definitely qualified.

Forgive us our debts as we forgive our debtors – Definitely work in progress, particularly when it came to Chip. But inch by grueling inch, I suppose progress was being made.

Lead us not into temptation but deliver us from evil – How many times had I come close to cashing it all in—the petulance, the stubbornness, my rebellion? And yet, he just wouldn't give up on me.

For yours is the kingdom, the power, and the glory forever – This wasn't in the version Yeshua quoted, but I read it later in Matthew. Either way, it was a bookend. Start off in praise, end up in praise. And all the parts in between? Well, as he said, it's been quite the journey.

I was interrupted by Yeshua raising his voice and calling out to the group. "But you will receive power when the Holy Spirit comes upon you."

The small band nodded. Whether they understood or not made little difference. They would soon enough.

"And you will be my witnesses in Jerusalem, and in all Judea and Samaria, and to the ends of the earth."

Once again they nodded.

And then, to their amazement, to *my* amazement, Yeshua's feet lifted from the ground and he started rising into the air. I watched in astonishment. A handful cried out in alarm, but he just kept rising . . . until slowly, one by one, they dropped to their knees. It seemed a pretty good idea and I followed suit, bowing my head and closing my eyes in a reverence I knew I had lacked far too often.

Eventually I heard Amber's ring on my phone. I opened my eyes to see I was kneeling in the prison's parking lot. Quickly gathering myself, hoping I'd not been spotted by security cameras, I rose, brushed off my slacks, and pulled out the phone.

"You okay?" I asked.

"The neatest thing just happened."

"Yeah?" I started walking toward the main entrance. "What's that?"

"She just pulled up in her car."

"Who's that? Who pulled up?"

"Aunt Cindy. Isn't that cool?"

I stopped in my tracks as she continued. "She's moving back in . . . Isn't that cool?"

"Uh—can you put her on?"

"She's unloading the car, just a sec."

I closed my eyes, took a deep breath and resumed walking. *Dear God,* I repeated my ongoing mantra, *what are you doing now?* The thought barely formed before I heard Yeshua's final words, as clearly as if I was still in the group:

"Behold . . . I am with you always."

Soli Deo gloria

Commune
Rendezvous with GOD
Volume Three

DISCUSSION QUESTIONS

CHAPTER ONE

Not long ago I entered (kicking and screaming) the marvelous world of grandparenthood. Once I convinced myself I didn't have to be old to be a grandfather (I write fiction, remember?), I discovered what a gift it was to sit back and marvel as I watched her explore life. Sadly, I missed some of these moments with my own daughters as I was far too busy and self-absorbed "building God's kingdom." Of course, that's important, but over the decades I've realized slowing down and enjoying the gifts of little moments is just as important in my relationship with him as moving mountains. I'm finally learning to sip and savor his goodness instead of quickly gulping it down so I can get to his "real work."

1. Do you agree that adoring him in "little blessings" is just as important as accomplishing "great and mighty things" for him? Why or why not?

2. For further insight and just for fun, take the other position and disagree with yourself regarding the above question.

3. What are some practical ways of slowing down and enjoying him in those little moments?

CHAPTER TWO

Jesus's insistence we call God "Father" was revolutionary. Even today the concept of this intimacy is so foreign we often elevate the very word, *Father*, into something more aloof and formal. Yet Jesus talks about an intimacy so deep our Father even knows the hairs on our head.

As the young men I mentor become fathers, I have great fun asking, "How's God messing with your theology?" Last week a first-time dad proudly held his two-week-old son up to the Zoom camera for us all to see. I asked him in one word to describe how he felt. But because we overuse the word *love*, it was the one word I told him he could not use. He thought a long moment and finally said: "Devoted." We all grew silent. Pause and chew on that a moment. If we, being imperfect parents, feel devotion toward our children, how much deeper devotion does God feel toward us?

1. To what degree to you understand the depth of God's devotion to you?

2. How can you grow in that understanding?

3. And, on a slightly different track, Yeshua says: "In order to grow, pain is necessary, suffering is optional." What does that mean?

CHAPTER THREE

I'm good with big trials. Honest. It's the pin-pricks that drive me crazy. I'm "too Christian" to swear but, boy, does that same anger run through my mind when I'm enjoying a great meal and bite a chunk out of my cheek—or if I'm in a hurry to get to work and I hit every single red light along the way and barely miss the jack(*a-hem*) donkey who pulls in front of me driving 12 mph.

1. Romans 8:28 says, "All things work together for the good to those who love the Lord and are called according to his purpose." Not some things, not most things, but *all* things. How would life be different if you really believed that?

2. How is it possible to keep your peace amidst the paper-cuts of life?

CHAPTER FOUR

Wrath. Punishment. Discipline. Pretty scary action from a God who is love (1 John 4:8). In this chapter, Will sees how wrath and love are interwoven, but . . .

1. What about punishment? How is that part of God's love?

2. What about discipline?

3. Is punishment the same as discipline? What's the difference?

4. How do these fit with Romans 8:1–2? "Therefore, there is now no condemnation for those who are in Christ Jesus, because through Christ Jesus the law of the Spirit who gives life has set you free from the law of sin and death."

CHAPTER FIVE

1. Religious chains come in all sorts of sizes. What are Patricia's chains?

2. What are yours?

3. What are the good things about "religion"?

4. How can religion become a prison whose captives need to be set free?

CHAPTER SIX

It's been said Christians may be the only Bible people read.

1. Where do you succeed at being God's sermon in shoes? Where do you fail?

2. Not long ago a friend who is a committed follower of Christ said, "If God has enemies, I'm entitled to them

too." The phrase left me speechless. As followers of Jesus, where is the flaw in that statement?

3. Who were Jesus's absolute worst enemies and how did he respond?

CHAPTER SEVEN

In this chapter both Darlene and Patricia's actions cause people to judge them incorrectly. No one knows their inner struggles. In Matthew 7:1–4 we read what Jesus says about judging.

> *"Do not judge, or you too will be judged. For in the same way you judge others, you will be judged, and with the measure you use, it will be measured to you. Why do you look at the speck of sawdust in your brother's eye and pay no attention to the plank in your own eye? How can you say to your brother, 'Let me take the speck out of your eye,' when all the time there is a plank in your own eye?"*

But the very next verse is one people often neglect:

> *"You hypocrite, first take the plank out of your own eye, and then you will see clearly to remove the speck from your brother's eye"* (v. 5).

Not exactly a call to remain complacent and let those we love continue to sin. And while we're quoting Scripture, let's not forget Hebrews 10:24:

> *"And let us consider how we may spur one another on toward love and good deeds.*

Spurring—not exactly turning a blind eye to sin. So—

1. How do you find the balance?

For me, I've discovered when I can't wait to tear into someone for their failures, I should probably check my heart and shut my mouth. But when I don't want to confront them, that's probably when I should. Why? My motives will be more out of love for them than my self-righteous ego.

CHAPTER EIGHT

1. How did Jesus not answering the beggar's prayers help them refine what they really missed and wanted?

2. How does God's refusal to immediately answer your prayers help you dig deeper to see your real need?

CHAPTER NINE

1. Yeshua is definitely raising the stakes for Will's growth. Have you seen him do it in your own life? Explain.

2. Remember these verses James wrote when first-century Christians were being tortured to death:

> *"Consider it pure joy, my brothers and sisters, whenever you face trials of many kinds, because you know that the testing of your faith produces*

> *perseverance. Let perseverance finish its work so that you may be mature and complete, not lacking anything."* James 1:2–4

3. What specific ways are you currently becoming "mature and complete, not lacking anything"?

4. And how does this tie in with Romans 8:28?

CHAPTER TEN

True vs. truth. Have you ever been so caught up in what's true that you've forgotten the truth?

1. Great thinkers often say understanding life is seeing it in "context, context, and more context."

2. What current examples can you think of where folks have lost track of the forest because of the trees?

CHAPTER TWELVE

Isn't passive-aggressiveness interesting? We can hide our frustration toward God all we want, but eventually, sometimes in the smallest detail, he finds a way of revealing us to ourselves.

1. When's the last time you've honestly let God know you were frustrated with him?

2. The Psalms are full of those emotions. Do one or two come to mind?

3. By the end, how does the psalmist often deal with his frustrations toward God? How does that apply to us?

CHAPTER FOURTEEN

The Joseph Namaliu character is based upon a good friend of mine I first met when filming a documentary of him overseas. I've changed enough details so I don't embarrass him (since he really is as shy and humble as in the book), but the resurrection of the baby is as close to the actual events as those I interviewed remember.

1. What are your thoughts about modern-day Christians performing miracles like that?

2. Why does God heal some people and not others?

CHAPTER SIXTEEN

Every summer I would direct a children's film in the Midwest. And every summer I'd attend my producer's ultra-faith church. Good people, deeply in love with Christ. But they refused any medical treatment, insisting God would heal. Sometimes he did. Sometimes he didn't. My heart broke over the couple who lost their baby because they refused medical care. They were four-way victims. They 1) lost their child 2) felt overwhelming guilt for "not having enough faith" 3) were judged by some in the church who felt they didn't have enough faith 4) and had to deal with the anger of locals and the authorities.

1. What does the Yeshua character mean in saying Patricia has the wrong kind of faith?

2. What does he mean about having "faith in faith" as opposed to faith in God?

3. Have you ever found yourself practicing that type of faith?

CHAPTER SEVENTEEN

I still marvel at Jesus's claims. "I am the Bread of Life." "I am the Living Water." "I am the Light of the world." My favorite is John 8 when he not only claims to have existed before Abraham but calls himself "I am," as God did when he appeared to Moses in the burning bush. No wonder, in the very next verse, they picked up rocks and tried to stone him to death.

But back to being the Bread of Life. I made a decision in college to read a little bit of the Bible every morning. *Not a lot*, usually just until I hit something profound. Then I'd stop and think and pray about it. Nothing in the past fifty years of my walk with him has made more of an impact than this little exercise. People point to my friendship with God as if it's some great gift. Nothing could be further from the truth. It's the simple fact that the more I hang out with him, even if it's a little each day, the greater our friendship grows.

1. How often do you allow your soul to feed upon God?

2. An obvious question, but what's more beneficial to our bodies—binging, gorging, then starving for days, or simply eating in daily moderation?

3. What are some *very practical and specific* steps you could take to develop a healthy eating pattern?

CHAPTER EIGHTEEN

I mentioned this in *Rendezvous with God - Volume One*, but it might be worth repeating: I'm not a fan of fasting—I get cranky, headachy, and unlike my more devout friends, I find the whole experience miserable. And yet Jesus said in Matthew 6, "*When* you fast" not "*If* you fast." Folks say it cleans toxins from their bodies, helps them focus on the spiritual. For me, it's simply an act of obedience, of telling my body to sit down, be quiet, and set the time aside for God. So, reluctantly, before each novel, I climb a hill and sit all day. Do I personally experience anything? Never. Except . . . One time I was walking home at the end of fasting over my novel *Fire of Heaven*, when a sudden realization struck. I'd spent the entire day telling God what I wanted the novel to accomplish, and never once asked what he wanted. I stopped dead in my tracks and confessed my stupidity. And instantly, wave after wave of thoughts rushed into my mind—so quickly I broke out laughing, "Wait, wait, hold on a second." I giggled as I fumbled for my pen and paper to write them all down. And yes, they made it into the novel—the most concentrated section in the entire trilogy. But all those other times? I felt nothing. Just straight up obedience which, though I felt nothing, I trusted would somehow help infuse his Spirit into the writing. (And, if it matters, the e-mails I've received over the years seem to indicate it actually works!)

1. How serious do you take fasting?

2. Is it worth it, if you experience nothing this side of heaven?

3. Like the discipline of Scripture reading, if you wanted, how would you implement the practice of fasting into your life?

CHAPTER NINETEEN

1. Over my half century with the Lord, I've tried just about everything Will tried twisting God's arm. What have you tried? Which ones seem to work?

2. Earlier, Jesus pointed out that it's better to pray with God than pray at him. What does that mean?

3. How different would we make our requests to Jesus if we really believed he was as close and intimate as a best friend sitting in the room beside us?

CHAPTER TWENTY

The church reader board Will passed read: "Sacrifice of Praise." My best friend died from an excruciating illness. It was thirty years ago, yet I'll never forget racing him to the hospital one night when he was bent over in the front seat of my car quietly, gasping, "Praise you, God. Bless you,

Jesus." The memory still brings a lump to my throat. For him, praise was truly a sacrifice. And, for the record, quite a few gave their life to Christ at his memorial service. But what about our normal, day-to-day life? Hebrews 13:15 says, "Through Jesus, therefore, let us continually offer to God a sacrifice of praise—the fruit of lips that openly profess his name."

1. How often is the sacrifice of praise a part of your life?

2. If you wanted to increase that time, what are some practical, doable steps to accomplish it?

CHAPTER TWENTY-TWO

Some folks aren't thrilled about this portion of the Lord's Prayer: "Lead us not into temptation but deliver us from evil." To be honest, I don't quite understand the first part unless it's asking God to steer me away from opportunities of sin. But the second part I understand loud and clear. I can't begin to count the number of times he's delivered me from evil. Occasionally when I'm looking for things to thank him for, I'll simply recall those times he's stopped me from willfully jumping into a pit that looks like great swimming on the surface but is full of deadly vipers.

1. What about you? Can you recall times he's saved you from yourself?

CHAPTER TWENTY-FOUR

Four decades ago, when I attended film school in Rome, I saw a motion picture I'll never forget. Over there it was titled, *Never Give an Inch*. In it one man was pinned in water as another tried keeping him alive in much the same manner as this chapter. The analogy was too good to pass up—particularly when it came to being filled with God's breath and spreading it to others.

Often, when depression, anger, or self-pity creep at my door, God puts someone in my path who needs help. What a smart way of getting me to take my eyes off me. And, more often than not, when his "streams of living water" pour out of me onto another, *I* get soaked in the process.

1. What times in your life has your "cup runneth over" onto others and then onto yourself?

CHAPTER TWENTY-FIVE

I have two verses on the wall in front of my desk. The first, is from 1 Thessalonians 5:16–18:

> *Rejoice always, pray continually, give thanks in all circumstances; for this is God's will for you in Christ Jesus.*

I suppose if there's a life verse, that's it. The second, right above it on the wall, is the portion from Isaiah 55:9–11 that Will read in our story:

> *"As the heavens are higher than the earth, so are my ways higher than your ways and my thoughts than your thoughts. As the rain and the snow come down from heaven, and do not return to it without watering the earth and making it bud and flourish, so that it yields seed for the sower and bread for the eater, so is my word that goes out from my mouth: It will not return to me empty, but will accomplish what I desire and achieve the purpose for which I sent it."*

1. What would happen in our lives if we really, I mean *really*, believed those verses?

My favorite kid's book series (which may be why it's my most obscure) is titled The Imager Chronicles. In one of the episodes the kids visit The Weaver of Creation. They see him at a loom weaving a dark thread into a friend's life. They don't understand that it will make her life a tapestry of depth and beauty. And by trying to stop him, they nearly destroy her.

2. What dark threads has the Weaver woven into your tapestry?

3. How do they bring out your depth and beauty in becoming his masterpiece?

CHAPTER TWENTY-SIX

No question here, just another incredible promise by Jesus to chew on:

> *"Which of you fathers, if your son asks for a fish, will give him a snake instead? Or if he asks for an egg, will give him a scorpion? If you then, though you are evil, know how to give good gifts to your children, how much more will your Father in heaven give the Holy Spirit to those who ask him!"* (Luke 11:11–12)

A sample from the next installment:

INSIGHT

Rendezvous with GOD
Volume Four

STANDING AT THE stern of the ferry on the way home, I gripped and regripped the cold, wet railing. *Call EMS . . . Sitting on a powder keg . . . You know how they get?* What had I gotten myself into? First day on the job and I nearly lost my life. Okay, maybe that's a slight exaggeration. Or was it?

"Rough day at the office?"

I turned to see Yeshua in his trademark robe and sandals, wind tugging at his hair.

I didn't bother hiding my sarcasm. "You think?"

He remained silent as we looked out over the channel—the water heaving in slow gray swells, clouds black and heavy with rain. After another moment, he spoke. "Remember, how I promised this would be your greatest adventure?"

I scoffed. "Lockdowns, teaching what I don't know, prisoners convicted for God knows what."

"And whom I deeply love."

"You love everybody."

"Like Father, like Son."

I looked back over the water. "You've been taking me on 'adventures' since the day we met. But this one—I'm not so sure."

"Have you ever been?"

He had me there.

"That's why it's called faith."

I nodded, not thrilled with the answer. "So what's in store for me this time?"

"Only if you agree."

"Free will," I quoted a phrase he often used.

"Always."

"And if I say no?"

"I'll still love you. You won't reach your fullest potential, but you'll always have my love."

"And my fullest potential is . . ."

He tilted back his head and quoted, "'*To become whole and complete, lacking in nothing.*'"

I snorted at the impossibility.

He ignored me and continued. "All this time you've allowed the Spirit to grow inside you—love, peace, righteousness. And I couldn't be prouder."

I glanced down at the railing, never quite sure how to accept compliments from the Son of God.

He continued, "But it's all been from the inside out."

"Spiritual transformation," I said. "That's what you've called it."

"God's Spirit inside you doing the heavy lifting. If you tried it on your own, you'd just turn religious on me. And then we'd have to deal with all the judgment and pride nonsense."

I nodded, seeing that in enough people's lives, including my own.

"But now with my Spirit, you have springs of living water inside you."

"Springs of . . ."

"Life. My life. My love, peace, and whether you care to admit it or not—joy." (For the record, we had plenty of past discussions regarding my inner-Eeyore.)

"My Spirit's inside you, pushing back on all the outside pressure."

"Your balloon analogy," I said. "From our first meetings."

"You remembered?

"Remember? I've been writing about it."

"Your book?"

"Books," I said, a bit sheepishly. "Looks like there'll be more than one."

He chuckled. "You've always been an overachiever. Just as well. And the sooner the better."

"Meaning?"

He gave no answer, but said, "It's time for those springs of living water to flow out of you, so others can start drinking from them."

I paused, thinking it through. "Is that why Cindy, my ex, is coming home, thinking she can move back in with me?"

"Along with her boyfriend."

"Boyfriend!?"

"Spoiler alert. Sorry."

I bit my tongue, figuring it's best not to swear in God's company. "And my niece? And her baby? And that piece of work called, Chip?"

"And don't forget Darlene and Patricia."

"And this prison thing too?"

"Stay calm. Buckle in."

"You're dropping me in the middle of a roaring freeway telling me to stay calm!"

"Keep your arms and hands in the vehicle at all times."

"That's not very—"

"And whatever you do, don't get out and push."

"Push?"

"At the speed we're traveling, you'll only wind up hurting yourself."

"So what am I *supposed* to do?"

"Just believe."

"Believe?"

"Kick back and enjoy the ride. Let me do the driving."

I closed my eyes, searching for patience, when the ferry shuddered and lunged. I reopened them just in time to see a giant wave crashing down upon us. I reached for the railing but there was no railing. It had vanished into the dark. *Dark?* I panicked, groping for anything until I found a rope stretched from the deck to the mast. *Mast?* I peered through the driving rain and saw we were back on the disciples' boat—in the middle of the night—in a raging storm! Yeshua was standing beside me. Not exactly standing. He was three feet away, outside the boat, standing on the water.

"Seriously?" I shouted.

He shrugged.

Another wave washed over us. I came out of it choking and coughing. When I caught my breath, I turned to him and shouted, "We're back in Galilee!"

He pointed to the other side of the boat where his frightened disciples were huddled in the wind, yelling at the big man I'd come to know as Peter. He was straddled over the edge of the vessel, one foot on the deck, the other foot in the water.

"Are you out of your mind?" they were shouting. "Get back here! Don't be a fool!"

I called to Yeshua. "Is this where he walks on water?"

He motioned for me to keep watching as the men continued to yell, pleading for Peter to come to his senses. Someone grabbed Peter's arm, but he yanked it away and turned back to the lake.

And then, not thirty feet away, barely visible through the wind and rain, I saw Yeshua again—motioning for Peter to come out and join him.

I turned back to where Yeshua had been. He was there, as well. "That's you!" I yelled.

He nodded for me to continue watching.

I turned to see Peter now standing with both feet on the water—not *in* the water but *on* it—just like the Yeshua beside me. He was clinging to the side of the boat for all he was worth, as it rose and fell with each swell, but clearly standing . . . while, in the distance, through the driving rain, the other Yeshua motioned for him to come out and join him.

The big man was terrified, but he was determined. Slowly, he inched his foot forward, testing the water's firmness, until he'd stretched it out enough to take a step. Now he had a choice. Put his weight on that foot and lean forward, or do the sensible thing and pull back.

The men continued yelling at him to do the sensible thing.

But, keeping his eyes riveted on Yeshua, he shifted his weight to the front foot and released his grip on the boat.

The men gasped. Everyone froze, including Peter as they watched and waited.

He remained standing.

The Yeshua beside me shouted, "That's my boy!"

Then, as unsteady as a toddler taking his first step, Peter brought his rear foot forward. Wind ripped at his robe, rain and water blew into his face, but he kept his eyes locked on Yeshua until both feet were together, side by side—separated for balance, but together. When it was clear he wasn't sinking, he stretched out his first foot, put his weight on it as before and moved ahead. Another wave broke over the boat drenching us. I expected the same to happen with Peter. But to my astonishment, he rose on the wave like a cork then settled back safely into the trough—as he completed his second step, then a third, each more confident than the last.

I turned to the Yeshua beside me. "That's amazing!"

"Want to give it a try?"

"Me?"

He grinned.

"We tried that once," I shouted. "Back on the beach, remember?"

"You were a rookie. Welcome to the majors."

"I . . . don't know how?"

"Neither does Pete." He nodded back to the scene before us. "Just keep your eyes on me."

"I don't—"

Suddenly I was standing on the water—exactly where Peter had been, between the boat and the other Yeshua. Only now there was no Peter and it was the Yeshua who had been beside me.

"No problem, Will!" he shouted. "You've got this."

I saw a wave coming at us and braced myself. But, like Peter, when it hit, I simply rose and fell with it. I looked down to see I was actually standing on water. How was that possible? I searched for the logic—not to mention a little courage.

Yeshua read my mind and shouted, "You don't need those! Just believe!"

I looked up to him and he nodded in encouragement. Then, against all common sense (and the hope people don't die from hallucinations) I moved my foot forward, slow and cautious, before putting my weight on it. The surface was more spongy than firm, like a foam mattress. But it held.

"There you go!"

I nodded. Took a breath. And then I took another step. Once again, it held.

"See!" he shouted. "A piece of cake!"

I started my third step when I heard the men shouting behind me. I turned to see a killer wave coming directly at us.

"No!" Yeshua shouted. "On me! Keep your eyes on me!"

But the wave was huge. I wiped the water from my face and looked down. What was I doing?"

"Me, Will!" Yeshua shouted. "On me!"

I was no Peter. I couldn't do this.

The wave hit and covered me. When it passed I was no longer on top of the water. Not entirely. I'd sunk to my calves. I panicked, trying to pull them up, but I only sank deeper until the water wrapped around my knees. Then my thighs.

"Will!"

I kept sinking. The water was at my waist. "Help me! I can't . . ." Then my chest.

I kicked and thrashed, but my coat had become a straitjacket, my shoes lead weights until, despite every effort, I was dragged under. I looked up to the surface moving further and further away. There was nothing I could do—until I felt a hand grab my wrist and pull.

Instantly, I was back on the deck of the ferry, gasping for breath, my hands clutching the railing. I turned to Yeshua but he was gone. Only his voice remained, four fading words. "Why do you doubt . . .?"

Previous Praise for Bill Myers's Novels

Blood of Heaven

"With the chill of a Robin Cooke techno-thriller and the spiritual depth of a C. S. Lewis allegory, this book is a fast-paced, action-packed thriller." —Angela Hunt, *NY Times* best-selling author

"Enjoyable and provocative. I wish I'd thought of it!" —Frank E. Peretti, *This Present Darkness*

ELI

"The always surprising Myers has written another clever and provocative tale." —Booklist

"With this thrilling and ominous tale, Myers continues to shine brightly in speculative fiction based upon biblical truth. Highly recommended." —*Library Journal*

"Myers weaves a deft, affecting tale." —*Publishers Weekly*

The Face of God

"Strong writing, edgy . . . replete with action . . ." —*Publishers Weekly*

Fire of Heaven

"I couldn't put the *Fire of Heaven* down. Bill Myers's writing is crisp, fast-paced, provocative . . . A very compelling story." —Francine Rivers, *NY Times* best-selling author

Soul Tracker

"Soul Tracker provides a treat for previous fans of the author but also a fitting introduction to those unfamiliar with his work. I'd recommend the book to anyone, initiated or not. But be careful to check your expectations at the door . . . it's not what you think it is." —Brian Reaves, *Fuse* magazine

"Thought provoking and touching, this imaginative tale blends elements of science fiction with Christian theology." —*Library Journal*

"Myers strikes deep into the heart of eternal truth with this imaginative first book of the Soul Tracker series. Readers will be eager for more." —*Romantic Times* magazine

Angel of Wrath

"Bill Myers is a genius." —Lee Stanley, producer, Gridiron Gang

Saving Alpha

"When one of the most creative minds I know gets the best idea he's ever had and turns it into a novel, it's fasten-your- seat-belt time. This one will be talked about for a long time." —Jerry B. Jenkins, author of *Left Behind*

"An original masterpiece." —Dr. Kevin Leman, best-selling author

"If you enjoy white-knuckle, page-turning suspense, with a brilliant blend of cutting-edge apologetics, *Saving Alpha* will grab you for a long, long time." —Beverly Lewis, *NY Times* best-selling author

"I've never seen a more powerful and timely illustration of the incarnation. Bill Myers has a way of making the gospel accessible and relevant to readers of all ages. I highly recommend this book." —Terri Blackstock, *NY Times* best-selling author

"A brilliant novel that feeds the mind and heart, *Saving Alpha* belongs at the top of your reading list." —Angela Hunt, *NY Times* best-selling author

"*Saving Alpha* is a rare combination that is both entertaining and spiritually provocative. It has a message of deep spiritual significance that is highly relevant for these times." —Paul Cedar, Chairman, Mission America Coalition

"Once again Myers takes us into imaginative and intriguing depths, making us feel, think and ponder all at the same time. Relevant and entertaining. *Saving Alpha* is not to be missed." —James Scott Bell, best-selling author

The Voice

"A crisp, express-train read featuring 3D characters, cinematic settings and action, and, as usual, a premise I wish

I'd thought of. Succeeds splendidly! Two thumbs up!"
—Frank E. Peretti, *This Present Darkness*

"Nonstop action and a brilliantly crafted young heroine will keep readers engaged as this adventure spins to its thought- provoking conclusion. This book explores the intriguing concept of God's power as not only the creator of the universe, but as its very essence." —Kris Wilson, *CBA* magazine

"It's a real 'what if ?' book with plenty of thrills . . . that will definitely create questions all the way to its thought-provoking finale. The success of Myers's stories is a sweet combination of a believable storyline, intense action, and brilliantly crafted, yet flawed characters." —Dale Lewis, TitleTrakk.com

The Seeing

"Compels the reader to burn through the pages. Cliff-hangers abound, and the stakes are raised higher and higher as the story progresses—intense, action-shocking twists!" —Title Trakk.com

When the Last Leaf Falls

"A wonderful novella . . . Any parent will warm to the humorous reminiscences and the loving exasperation of this father for his strong-willed daughter . . . Compelling characters and fresh, vibrant anecdotes of one family's faith journey." —*Publishers Weekly*

BILL MYERS

Rendezvous with GOD

a novel

BILL MYERS

a novel

Temptation

Rendezvous with God Volume Two